Tiburones

Perry Robert Wilkes

Liberación Press

Published in the United States of America by Liberación Press.

ISBN 9781735011554
1.   Fiction, General
2.   Mexico
3.   Sea of Cortez
4.   Expats

Liberación Press
P.O. Box 6460
Nogales, AZ 85628

Cover and book design by Carolyn Kinsman.
Printed in the United States of America by IngramSpark.

There's zero correlation between being
the best talker and having the best ideas.
— Susan Cain

All journeys have secret destinations of
which the traveler is unaware.
– Martin Buber

Fiction is the lie through which we tell
the truth.
– Albert Camus

Dedication and Disclaimer:
The Good, the Bad and the Sloppy*

Nobody really knows who wrote *On the Sublime*. It's a treatise on writing that's sometimes attributed to Cassius Longinus (c. 213-273 AD), although he was most likely not the author. But whoever wrote it listed five sources of sublimity:

> "great thoughts, strong emotions, certain figures of thought and speech, noble diction, and dignified word arrangement."

And with any luck, you'll find little of that in this volume.

This is a work of fiction, a side-eyed glance at the foibles, fumbles, and humanity of well-meaning folk adapting to a markedly different culture in Mexico than what they left behind after crossing the border. Most of them did their best to leave things better than they found them before they also passed beyond the great veil to make a space for the next person.

This book is dedicated to the people of a little coastal town on the Sea of Cortez that closely resembles a place called Bahía Tiburón.

> The Moving Finger writes; and, having writ,
> Moves on: nor all thy Piety nor Wit
> Shall lure it back to cancel half a Line,
> Nor all thy Tears wash out a Word of it.
> – *The Rubáiyát of Omar Khayyam*
> *(Edward Fitzgerald translation; 1859)*

(* The author has spent many hours pouring over the words herein to avoid any sloppy errors, and he hopes it was not in vain. But any remaining errors are his fault alone.)

TABLE OF CONTENTS...LIST OF TALES

Juan brought Robert a copy of his new menu so Robert could check the English translations for his new little taco stand, his *puesto*. Robert scanned the items and almost choked when he got to the translation for *Jaiba al Diablo*. Juan was enthusiastic but he was never a good proofreader and he tended to skip over things. There were even misspellings in his Spanish, but Robert thought that was charming and didn't correct most of them. But this translation read, "Deviled Crap," and he thought he should speak up. Juan knew it was good to have Robert look over his work but he always resented him finding anything wrong. And when Robert hooted at something on the menu, Juan got annoyed. At first he didn't see the problem until Robert fully explained it, and then he admitted it would be a good change.

1

R obert had settled into a nice chair on the veranda with a second cup of hot coffee and the local newspaper to practice his Spanish, and Liz was in her study working on her latest drawing. As usual, they had arisen as dawn broke over the Sea, and then the two lights in the kitchen had flickered and gone out. So now the electricity was off all over town. Again. It was a warm morning in Springtime, and another normal day in the quiet little town of Bahía Tiburón, where the electricity is always tentative and people accept that as part of the price of living in exotic places. Somehow, it adds to the charm—at least if you're a gringo, retired or otherwise, with extra time on your hands. For the local folks trying to cope with life and make a living, maybe not so much. Robert's friend Juan once told him, "I always thought I was just another *pobre Mexicano* trying to scratch out a living here in this desolate country and I never knew I was 'exotic' until you pointed that out for me."

Robert paused for a moment before reading to look out over the Sea of Cortez, the famous Sea of Cortez, that glistened in the clear desert sun. It still amazed him and Liz that they'd somehow managed to buy a nice piece of beachfront property with an old house on it anywhere in the world, but especially on a quiet beach in Mexico. And now the Sea stretched almost from the foot of his veranda clear to the horizon, where he could just see a few sections of the distant Baja Peninsula. Robert and Liz hadn't been over there in a few years, but the memories were still vivid, of taking that big ferry from Topolobampo to La Paz, and the two months they spent making their way slowly back north to the border at San Diego. And that's when they realized there was nothing, absolutely nothing, overrated about retirement.

They had been together, "happily unmarried,"as Robert liked to say, for more than thirty years now, and it had been good for them both. Liz could always remember how many years they'd been together, exactly, and it was more than all their earlier and failed marriages put together. It had taken a while in their early years to get the whole idea of relationship right, but they had finally figured it out together and it just kept working well for them. Neither of them could remember the exact date, or even the month, when they decided to move in together (or "shack up," as Robert put it), but it was sometime in May or June. So they picked a date each year and declared that as their anniversary. And they kept Valentines Day as a second anniversary (a back-up, of sorts) because it was a nice idea and easy to remember.

The horizon that Robert now enjoyed from his veranda had its own special moments in history and he could even imagine that old trawler named the Western

Flyer, from Monterrey, California, out there chugging south across the water on its way back to Monterrey in the Spring of 1940. It was the boat that carried John Steinbeck and Doc Ricketts on a rollicking trip to Mexico that Steinbeck chronicled in his colorful book, *The Log of the Sea of Cortez*. Sometimes Robert wished he could have been on that boat, back then when the Sea was raw and wild and very few people lived on her shores. It was still a tempestuous body of water that deserved respect, but Steinbeck and those guys had to pack almost all their supplies aboard for a month or so at sea. Especially their beer. And a month's supply of beer can take up a lot of space on a boat.

But after twenty years of living on these shores, Robert had managed to gather his own ragtag collection of memories about the Sea of Cortez—since the first time he and Liz crested that big dune overlooking a fabulous sweeping view of Bahía Tiburón and the islands beyond. That famous "Holy moly!" moment that astounds every new visitor and that old-timers never get tired of. And as he relaxed in the warm morning light he could recall a few of the incidents that got them here. Like that guy they met on a windy day in March behind the dunes down in San Carlos, just before they got to Tiburón.

***

José

Let's call him José.

Robert didn't know his real name because they never actually introduced themselves. It was the middle of the afternoon when José emerged from the stubby landlocked mangrove tangle inshore of the high coastal dunes north of San Carlos. Seagulls were cruising overhead and calling in the breeze when José looked around and saw Robert and Liz. He was still zipping his fly when he turned and smiled, and started walking toward them.

Robert and Liz were sitting on the sand leaning against the side of their car, absorbed in reading their books, with the sound of breaking waves on the Sea of Cortez just over the tall wind-sculpted dunes. It was March, there was a cold north breeze blowing along the coast, and they were hunkered down wearing their jackets on the south side of the car in the warm rays of the Mexican sun as gusts of wind sprinkled them with bits of sand. Robert glanced up briefly from his book toward the tall and distinctive volcanic mountain that stands a few miles south of where he was sitting, the mountain called *Tetas de Cabra*. Goat tits. And that's when he saw José.

José approached them smiling broadly, and Robert thought, "Here we go again. Here comes another scam." An American in the *turista* zone is assumed to be rich—or at least gullible. And, compared to the average Mexican, the gringos are pretty well off. But Robert knew that as soon as they returned to the U.S. the mortgage payment was due, and the gas bill, and the water bill. And that they drove their old car to San Carlos because they didn't have the money to fly. Yet none of that matters. At least they had a car that could make it all the way to San Carlos. And they had enough money for a cheap motel room. They even had enough to just hang out on the beach for a while. And to a lot of Mexicans, that looks pretty rich.

But as José drew closer, Robert decided to relax and just go with the situation. Anyway, his Spanish could use some practice. It always needed practice. It might also be be a good chance to learn more about the local culture, and Robert could always tell him "No," later on when he asked for money. Or maybe he would just give him a couple of bucks. It wouldn't really hurt to do that.

"Buenos dias," José said with a broad toothy grin. *"¿Tiene agua, por favor?"* He started off with a short detour by asking for water. On the way to asking for money.

"No, no tenemos agua." Robert closed his book and set it aside. They didn't have an extra drinking cup, and they sure didn't want to share theirs with a guy who hadn't washed his hands after holding his dong to take a whiz.

José looked troubled for a moment as he considered what his next angle would be. Then Robert said, *"Pero tenemos una cerveza, si quieres."*

"¡Pues si, como no!" His eyes brightened and his smile broadened considerably as he sat down nearby on the sand and Robert retrieved a cold bottle of Negra Modelo from the cooler. It was a decent way to share a little of the wealth. Robert had a full beer cooler. José had nothing.

He was of average height and build, and he was dressed in a dirty plaid long-sleeved shirt with the sleeves rolled up to his elbows. He wore dusty black jeans and a very old pair of lace-up hiking boots with badly-worn soles. He might have walked from town, and probably slept in the mangroves at night.

He would have been a reasonably handsome young man, but his most noticeable feature was a prominent scar that started at his forehead about an inch below the hairline and then ran across over his right eye and down his cheek. It looked like a terrible injury, and a miracle that he still had his right eye. The scar gave him a fearsome appearance, and Robert decided not to ask him about it.

He was from Guaymas, and he had come to nearby San Carlos looking for a job. With all the American *turistas* hanging out around this area, there was more work and the pay was better than in Guaymas. There might be some kind of menial restaurant or motel job available. It wouldn't be a skilled, high-paying job, but it would sure beat working on those decrepit shrimp boats rusting in the old harbor at Guaymas. Tourist-related jobs in

San Carlos were a lot more pleasant than a week or so at sea on a smelly, rolling shrimp boat, and they were a lot less dangerous.

José was a gregarious fellow, and soon he was telling Robert most of his life story. Liz occasionally smiled and looked up from her book, usually to help Robert with a Spanish word or phrase. José quickly drained the first beer, and Robert offered him a second as the story continued.

A few years ago, Jose had decided to go north to Tijuana, both for the adventure of it and to see what kind of job he could get. Before long, he was a decoy for a group of coyotes smuggling people across the border to the golden land of California.

His job was to cross the border at night...and get caught. He would slip through a hole in the fence, scramble up the embarkment, and sprint off into the dark California desert. Alarms would ring, and about a dozen Immigration agents, maybe with a helicopter or two overhead, would converge to capture him and haul him off to be processed. His job each night was to stay free as long as possible and keep the *migra* occupied.

In the middle of all this, an observer on the Tijuana side of the fence would radio a signal to the coyotes, and they would herd a group of paying customers across the border and into the night to rendezvous with a waiting truck or van. The next day, after the *migra* had tossed Jose back across the border, he'd collect his pay and wait for the next assignment.

The pay was decent and he enjoyed playing games with those overweight Immigration guys. Plus, they gave him a place to sleep overnight and a meal in the morning. But he was growing curious about that big, rich country to the north. There was a lot of talk about the high wages and the good times a young guy could have in L.A. Besides, now he had some pretty good ideas about how to dodge the *migra,* and it would just be a great adventure.

So late one night, long after the burning sun had settled into the vast Pacific Ocean, José slipped across the border, disappeared into the night, and worked his way north to the Big City.

Soon he had a job in L.A. making expensive magnesium muscle-car wheels for the teenagers of California in an illegal factory located somewhere in an old industrial district. He was delivered blindfolded each night to a large windowless building and kept there until his shift was over. The air inside was a poisonous soup of heavy metals, solvents and paint fumes, but he only planned to work there until he could afford to leave. It was a piecework job, and he was paid for each wheel he finished. Then another guy slapped a "Made in Brazil" sticker on it and sealed it in a box.

It was dangerous toxic work, but the pay was good, and before long he bought himself a used Ford pickup truck. He registered it in the name of the guy who owned the house where he rented a bedroom.

Then he quit the factory job and headed north to the Central Valley to pick vegetables. It was long, hard work, but he was working days now, outside in the fresh air far away from the toxic mag wheel factory. And he was making a lot more money than he'd made picking vegetables when he was a young kid in the large agribusiness fields a couple hundred miles south of Guaymas at Culiacán. He made enough, in fact, to rent a small, shabby apartment in a nearby town. Things were working out pretty well so far.

But late one night it all came to an end.

José was driving back to the apartment, and he was drunk after leaving a party in one of the small farming towns nearby. He passed out, ran off the road, and rolled his truck in a freshly plowed field. When he woke up in the hospital he had a nasty gash down his face and a lot of questions to answer.

As soon as they patched him up and let him out of the hospital, a couple of Immigration agents drove him south in the back of a government van, back to the border. The fun was over. He was headed home.

José drained his second beer and Robert dug into the bottom of the cooler to find another couple of cold ones. Robert rarely drank more than one beer at a sitting, and that's usually only with dinner. But he was on vacation and really didn't have anything better to do with the afternoon than lean against the car, nurse a second beer, and listen to José, who had been talking for quite a

while and was glad to see another cold bottle
headed his way. Robert got the impression that
José was used to drinking a lot more beer than he
was. They were now at sea level, and alcohol is a
lot less powerful at sea level than it is where he
and Liz normally lived, in New Mexico at the
southern end of the Rocky Mountains at about
5000 feet of elevation.

After a long swallow, José continued.

"You know," he said, "actually I'm glad to be
back in my own country. Back in Mexico. Back
where it's a free country and you can do whatever
you want!"

José saw Robert's incredulous look. There was a
halfway smile plastered across Robert's face and
his mouth was hanging open.

"Sure, there's a lot of money up there in the
United States," he continued, "but there are too
many damned regulations! They're always trying to
stop you from doing anything!"

This was one of the more interesting
observations about the U.S. that Robert had ever
heard. We Americans, he thought—we call
ourselves Americans, to the great annoyance of all
the other people who live in North, Central and
South America—are always beating our chests and
touting the "Land of the Free, the Home of the
Brave" as if there were no other free, or brave
people in the world. The shear size and wealth of
the US allows its people to be so ethnocentric—
and most of them spend their entire lives without

really thinking much about the rest of the world or other people's perspectives, or ever crossing the border. Robert could just imagine José at an American Legion convention telling them they were all oppressed. It would be a hoot.

But Robert had never before really recognized the essential libertarian nature of Mexico, and it was a revelation to him. There were, indeed, very few rules regarding public safety, sanitation, health, and a variety of other issues—as he understood it all in his limited gringo way. Or at least they weren't enforced. The health and safety standards of most of the United States—standards driven by a Northern European heritage—have long been considerably higher than those south of the border. To visit Mexico was always an adventure, a walk on the wild side. That was one of its attractions, and Robert hadn't thought much about how it came to be.

In his own country, Robert had always associated libertarianism with a childish shirking of responsibility: "I can do anything I want, and nobody can stop me! It doesn't matter if I throw my trash into the street and it all blows onto your property. That's your problem, not mine!"

That's the way it was. North of the border, at least. The rules were simple and clear, and violating them might not look very appealing to most people. But in Mexico, the same behavior seemed at least a little picturesque, a charming national characteristic. José had just given him something to think about.

José went on to say that he could build a rickety food stand out here on the beach if he wanted to, and nobody could stop him. He could sell hamburgers or tacos and beer if he wanted to and there was nobody to answer to, nobody to buy a license from, nobody to hassle him.

Robert wasn't sure the authorities would tolerate unlicensed beer sales on the beach, at least without paying somebody off, but he guessed there might be nobody to keep José from selling tainted food to the public. But if he did that and somebody died, a *pobre* like him could be tossed into prison to rot for the rest of his life. Maybe there would be a trial, and maybe there wouldn't. His responsibilities were minimal, and so were his rights. It would be his problem, not a problem of the larger society, and few people would care one way or the other. It would be tough luck for José. And for his victims, of course. And Robert guessed that's the way it goes.

José got up and thanked Robert and Liz for the beer before he wandered off toward another group of *gringos turistas* who were setting up a tent behind the dunes about a hundred yards away to dodge the cold northern winter that often sweeps down the Sea here in wintertime Sonora. Robert watched him walk away and sat there with the north breeze curling sand into rivulets beside his outstretched legs. He didn't know if José forgot to hit him up for some money or if he'd decided a couple of cold beers was payment enough for the entertainment.

Liz looked up as José left to try his luck elsewhere. Then she smiled and glanced at Robert, and went back to her reading.

"Hm," Robert said quietly, and mostly to himself, "Mexico. A free country."

***

2

A s the quiet morning Sea stretched out before him, Robert watched a cloud of pelicans, terns, and gulls diving onto a dark cloud of small fish that were moving westerly about 50 feet from the shoreline. The din of birds squawking and cackling filled the air. An occasional wave of white curled across the surface as small fish leaped from the water to escape a large fish feeding below. It's a hard life for those little fish that are the backbone of life here in one of the most fertile and productive seas of the world.

The strong cold northerly winds of Springtime had been especially long lasting—and very annoying—this year as the earth continued to rebalance and shrug off the profligate lifestyles of her careless human inhabitants. Sometimes the winds would blow for four or five days without stopping, an unheeded warning that Mother Nature would always be in charge no matter how much arrogance they inflicted on her.

While Robert and Liz did their best to conserve energy and resources, it seemed that much of humanity was invested in doing their best to mess things up. Robert measured his gas mileage in gallons per week, and took pride in every day that the car remained unused in the garage. Besides, it wasn't all that far to walk to the corner grocery, and he needed the exercise anyway. He might pay a premium here in Tiburón for things that were cheaper in Hermosillo, but the folks at the store needed to make a living, and they saved him the gas and time of a shopping trip to the big city.

And those strong cold northerlies that roar down all the valleys of the west had a special role here—in the biggest valley of the west—churning the Sea of Cortez and bringing nutrients to the surface. Winds and geography have no concern for the pathetic political boundaries of humanity. Whenever a large winter cold wave surges south from Canada the heavy air flows down through the low points, to sea level. It pours down the deserts and canyons of the inland west that are connected to the great rift system that created the Colorado River valley, the Imperial Valley, and Death Valley, where they converge and spill out onto the Sea of Cortez. And when the tide roars north into the Sea, directly into the opposing winds, it creates tall dangerous waves that mariners avoid. There's even a channel along the Baja that's named *Canal Salsipuedes*. It means "Get out if you can."

Robert looked out over that famous Sea at the small island that was halfway to the coast of Baja California, and he thought about the large trench deep under the water just on the other side of the island. The trench was part of the great San Andreas Fault system that long ago separated the Baja from the mainland of Mexico and that cleaves northward through California until it dives into the Pacific Ocean at Daly City, just west of San Francisco. And he recalled riding on the BART from San Francisco and seeing those "…little boxes made of ticky-tacky…" that comprised the housing of Daly City and aptly inspired that 1960s song by Malvina Reynolds. Robert and many of his friends back in the 1960s felt it would be no great loss if the next big earthquake to hit California resulted in ugly Daly City ending up in the Pacific Ocean. And now he sat here sipping coffee on his porch at the opposite end of the same fault line where he might well also end up in the drink. Robert was often afflicted with those kinds of mental wanderings and distractions.

The little island out there in the middle of the Sea was a volcano long ago at the edge of the Fault, and the trench beside it is several thousand feet deep. There are even hot spots at the bottom, with some of those strange life forms that you read about now and then. And there are also a lot of minerals and nutrition that settle down there and are available to fertilize the Sea. A couple of times every day the tides bring a surge of trillions of tons of Pacific sea water into the Sea of Cortez to scoop up that nutrition waiting on the bottom and spread it through the Midriff Islands where it enriches the microbes and plankton that feed the large schools of small fish. When a cold northerly roars down the Sea, it blows the surface water layer off and brings up even more of the nutrition. And the whole system builds from there.

Robert appreciated the beauty of a natural system that works so well, even if those Winter winds were an annoyance. The colonies of sea lions—*lobos del mar* in Spanish—and all the nesting birds who lived on the islands, had no idea of, or any interest in, the magic that gave them a livelihood as they continued in their quotidian ways, although human activity was now changing their world.

But when the cold winds abated it was the warm summer southerlies, the daily onshore breezes and the reciprocal nightly offshore breezes, that made this place wonderful—although it was the action of those cold northerlies that made it such a spectacularly fertile body of water. On their first visits during those long months of warm weather in the early fall, as they walked home in the evening down the middle of the town's deserted main street after a couple of large cold margaritas and a good seafood dinner, Robert and Liz decided to settle here. It was a happy accident when they found an old house on the beach that they could afford, one they could reimagine into a special place to live. The whole project became a memorable lesson in Mexican culture, and a challenge in its own right. And it left Robert with many stories to tell.

***

The Strange Saga of Francis' Tile Saw

I hope Francis doesn't find out what happened to his tile saw, Robert thought. At least not soon. I know it's inevitable, but I need more time to get my explanation together.

It all began when Francis, our seasonal neighbor two doors to the east, was kind enough to lend us his well used heavy-duty tile saw for our major remodeling job. It's one of those heavy saws that sits on a platform and uses water to cool the blade. It's the kind of saw that real professional tile-setters use, and it made our tile work far easier and more, dare we say it, professional looking, than we ever expected.

Over the course of several months, we cut a large number of tiles for various floors, walls, and countertops, and were about halfway through tiling the beachside veranda when the saw began to make some surprising noises. It sounded like bearing problems, and we suspected that maybe a few other things were going wrong deep in the bowels of The Monster. There was also the issue of the floppy blade guard held by a carriage bolt that had worn a groove into the aluminum housing; it now tilted precariously to the right and the nut was rusted solid to the bolt, making it impossible to tighten. The blade guard now leaned over so far that the blade itself was eating a long arc into it, adding yet another note to the increasing noise level. We jammed a small piece of wood into the dangerous-looking gap in an effort to keep the guard more or less level and free of the blade, but the time had come for some basic repairs.

It's a blistering-hot Friday morning in July when we decide to load it into the van and drive the 110 kilometers to Hermosillo on one of many hunting-and-gathering trips for construction supplies. We buy as much as we can in the *ferreteria*s of Tiburón, but we keep a continual list of things we need from the big city. With a population of almost a million, Hermosillo has most anything we can imagine we might need, although there are exceptions. And there's always something we need to add to the list— usually on the way back to Tiburón after we forgot to get it in Hermosillo.

This particular hot Friday is another in a long string of record-setting days. Outside the windows of our air-conditioned van the daily life of Sonora continues under a broiling desert sun. Vendors stand at major intersections in long pants, long-sleeved shirts, and hats, trying to hide from the sun as they sell *nopalito*s (chopped cactus*), durazno*s (peaches*), abanico*s (fans) or whatever else the market will bear. A friend of ours who works for the local natural gas company told us Hermosillo is the eighth hottest city in the world, and only slightly behind the other seven. It's the main reason they don't sell much gas for heating down here; most of it goes to the many local factories for industrial use. On this Friday, a temperature of 46 degrees C. (about 115 degrees F.) is predicted.

We pull into a tool store to see if they repair large tile saws and are given the name of Juan Carlos at *Taller Fimbres*. He seems to be the go-to guy for this kind of repair work and they recommend him highly. We call his number and find that his shop is at 72 Callejón Nogales, near Avenida Jose S. Healy. We head in that general direction while scanning the map to locate this particular *callejón,* or alley. Although it's listed in the index, it doesn't seem to appear on the map. We finally locate a short, unnamed alley that runs for two blocks just parallel to Avenida Healy, but the street sign says it's named Callejón Healy. We drive the entire area with no luck, and I joke, "Oh, everybody knows that Callejón Healy is really Callejón Nogales!" We have actually heard that sort of explanation before.

After more fruitless driving, we stop at a local *tienda* to ask the whereabouts of this elusive alley. Shopkeepers know their neighborhoods well; they sometimes need to make deliveries, and they know where their credit customers live. Liz goes in to ask while I wait in the car with the air conditioner running. Heat waves are shimmering above the street several blocks ahead of us. She emerges a few minutes later smiling wryly. "He said, 'Oh, everybody knows that Callejón Healey is really Callejón Nogales!'" Seems the name was changed a few years back and nobody has put up a new sign. In the scheme of budget priorities here, replacing incorrect or missing street signs, especially for an insignificant alley, ranks near the bottom. Add to that the custom of changing street names at the boundary of each new *colonia*, or neighborhood, and it makes for some interesting excursions in search of an address. But this is the sort of thing that never seems to strike the local people as unusual. It's just the way things are.

We finally arrive at 72 Callejón Nogales, a place we had actually passed a few times before in our search. Juan Carlos is sitting in a broken chair with a large spool of bright copper wire on the floor beside him, hand winding an armature for an electric motor. He's a young man, sporting a small ponytail, and there is some very good latin jazz on the stereo. A large fan is blowing hot air across his sweaty body. There are used electrical parts and pieces scattered on the floor and covering several shelves that line one wall. A pair of old couches and a sort of small kitchen are just across a large room beyond several large boxes of old, worn out drills. To the far left there is a makeshift bedroom. He turns off the music to take a quick look at our saw, saying he'll need a day to get it apart and give us a price for repairs.

We leave it with him, and after a few more errands it's time for lunch.

Often we'll go to one of the little sidewalk taco stands for some delicious fish tacos, but today we'll splurge. We stop at the Boulevard Café on Boulevard Kino near the *Zona Hotelera*, a nice little place that would stack up proudly against most restaurants in the US. And it's also well air-conditioned. I order the *huitlacoche* crepes and Liz has the quiche of the day. It doesn't get much better than this. Outside, a man washes our car for 30 pesos out of a bucket of dirty water. In this dusty environment it needs washing, even if the job isn't perfect. And he needs the money.

We go on about our errands, including the purchase of a pricey new diamond-tipped saw blade to replace the old one that wore out and started chipping the edges of the tiles.

There are also problems with the saw's water cooling system, but we think we can fix that. The little plastic y connector that directs water to both sides of the blade has fallen apart after many years in the sun, and Liz duct-taped the 1/4" plastic *mangueras* (hoses) together to keep the water flowing. It was ugly, it leaked really badly, yet it worked—after a fashion.

But it was time to look for a replacement. We take the pump and the taped-up hoses into a ferreteria and ask for a replacement piece. We're not surprised there's no such little plastic part available locally. But Mexicanos are very resourceful. The counterman pulls out a 1/4" copper elbow and a copper connector—the kind used on swamp coolers—and suggests we have a *soldaduria* weld it all together. He laughs and calls it a *mexicanada* just as a young woman walks by. She reproaches him for using that term, and he looks properly contrite as she walks away frowning. But he smiles and winks as we leave.

We look for a place that might specialize in such connections and end up at *Mangueras Ponce.* They have every imaginable kind of hose or tubing and they'll make up almost any kind of connector we need, but they don't have any little plastic Y fittings. Instead, they suggest using an inexpensive 1/4" copper tee, and it fits perfectly. We buy one and a few extras for spares, along with a couple meters of 1/4" plastic tubing for future repairs. Francis' saw has done a lot of hard work for us and we're ready to repay the favor by putting as many things as possible right again. After a long hot day of assorted other errands, we head for home.

On Saturday Juan Carlos calls with what he assumes is very bad news. The saw needs new bearings and brushes, and the armature needs cleaning. And yes he can fix the wobbly blade guard that was also causing problems. But the cost will be—he hesitates to say it—600 pesos (about US$55).

We're relieved at what sounds to us like a reasonable price for a major reconditioning job, and tell him to proceed. Juan Carlos is pleased that we've taken the news so well. The saw will be ready on Monday, and he'll be at the shop at 4:00 pm, after finishing various on-site jobs around the city. The timing works for us. It will be our last stop before heading due west on the narrow Tiburón highway well before sunset. All is good.

Over the weekend we find any number of jobs to keep us busy (we work in the early morning and late afternoon to avoid the crushing heat) but are very much looking forward to getting the saw back so we can continue working on the veranda. The details are coming together very nicely and we're anxious to see it finished. After eight months of continual construction, we're looking forward to seeing *anything* actually finished.

On a very hot Monday we head back to Hermosillo. Besides picking up the saw, we'll take care of a few leftover errands from the previous Friday. The heat wave continues. We've heard that this is the hottest summer since they started keeping records sixty years ago, and by early afternoon the A/C in the car is at its highest setting. At four o'clock we pull to the curb in front of Taller Fimbres to pick up the saw. Juan Carlos' wife is at the stove, fixing dinner in the heat as several fans move hot air through the room.

With a flip of the switch, the motor surges quietly into life. A set of new bearings and brushes and a reconditioned armature have worked wonders. The saw is spray-painted and looking better than we've ever seen it. And the blade guard no longer flops to one side. Juan Carlos proudly shows us that it is now welded to the frame to eliminate any further such problems. It's a very simple solution, and I briefly wonder why they hadn't done that originally, back at the factory. Then I remember that the blade guard is hinged in order to change the blade. Now there's no way to install our costly new blade. I gently explain this to Juan Carlos, and he is crestfallen.

We realize that somehow cutting the blade guard loose again will mess it up pretty badly and create other problems reattaching it. We study the situation for a better solution—or at least just a workable one. Hacking off the lower part of the guard to allow the blade to tilt and slide outward seems to be the only way to accomplish our goal, but we'll need to leave the little nipple where the water hose attaches. It suddenly appears likely that, instead of returning this tool in better shape than when we got it, we might instead be buying Francis a brand new, and very expensive, tile saw after we get through butchering this one. An old saying goes through my mind—the one about the road to hell being paved with good intentions.

To my surprise, Juan Carlos sets to work with a drill. He drills a number of holes on an arc and attempts to cut sideways to connect them. After he's created a godawful mess, and broken two drill bits, the word *mexicanada* comes back to mind. I suggest we go to the guy who did the welding job in the first place. At least he'll have some proper metalworking tools. We hope. Juan Carlos calls the welder on his cellphone then gives us the name and address, and he discounts his price by 50 pesos in an attempt to make amends. There is a palpable look of relief on his face as we drive away on the next leg of our latest adventure.

The welding shop is a small metal shed and a large shade structure. The yard is filled with car parts, motorcycle frames, and various other detritus. A huge Freightways semi-tractor sits astride the driveway. Reluctantly, we leave the cool comfort of the van to discuss our problem with Horatio, the welder. The air outside the van hits us like a blast furnace. Horatio agrees the only solution is to continue cutting away the blade guard with a metal grinder. While there is no way the saw is ever going to look even as good as it did just a few days ago, at least it now has the possibility of not being left with jagged and dangerous edges.

Horatio's brother José Luis, who owns the semi truck, sits under the shade structure enjoying one ice cold *cerveza* after another. As the afternoon temperature hovers at well over 100 degrees F, it looks like a rational way to deal with the shimmering heat of Hermosillo. He offers to share his chilled liquid provenance, but we decline. We still have a long drive back to Tiburón after this ordeal is over. Over the din of Horatio's grinding, José Luis tells me that he used to haul loads *en el otro lado,* (on the US side of the border) but now he prefers to drive the

Hermosillo-to-Mexicali route, through Caborca.
Other than beer, driving is the love of his life. He
also owns the brand new, and very large, Suzuki
motorcycle parked beside the truck, and enjoys
riding it through the streets of Hermosillo after
downing a few cold beers. Horatio, who is
sweating over the saw while we talk, is a
motorcycle racer, and the trophies on the back
wall of the storage shed are his. He's modifying a
motorcycle frame clamped onto the workbench
to get ready for the next race season.

Horatio grinds and shapes the edges, but the
blade still won't clear the water nipple. There's
some discussion of shortening the axle that carries
the blade but that sounds like a bad idea because
the retainer nut might come flying off. Instead, he
grinds an angle on one side of the axle to allow
the blade to clear the guard. It appears to be a
safe solution to the problem—one that still allows
plenty of attachment for the blade.

We finally load Francis' significantly modified
saw into the van, Horatio wipes the sweat from
his face, and I pay him 150 pesos (about $14US)
for his time, plus another 50 pesos to buy José
Luís some more beer. The sun draws near the
horizon and we begin our long drive home with
the sun in our faces, obscuring the road and the
oncoming traffic.

In the morning, our builder Miguel has a
couple of his strong young workers lift the heavy
saw onto its platform. He looks at the butchered

blade guard and shakes his head. After we tell him the story he smiles wryly, as he often does, and mutters the word *mexicanada*, as he walks away to deal with the morning's construction related problems. A couple of his crew took yesterday off, a practice referred to here as *San Lunes* (Holy Monday), and there's much work to do today.

We remove the battered blade that came with the saw and it comes off easily now, thanks to the angle-cut axle. Then we carefully unwrap the pricey new saw blade and fit it to the axle. Well almost. There's a one-inch diameter hole in the center of the blade but the axle measures only 5/8". This is not normally a problem, as saw blades always come with inserts of various sizes so they fit a variety of tools. But not this one. There are no inserts to be found in the package, and there's nothing around the house or garage that will suffice. There may well have been a little baggie containing inserts in the package at one time, but the package was not sealed and the baggie was probably "liberated" by someone with a similar problem.

At this point, I do the most logical thing. I ask Miguel if he might happen to have something that will fit. Mexicans generally assume that this is how the world works—that there will be no inserts in the package, and I think I already mentioned they are very resourceful. He replies that he probably has something at the house that will fit, and indeed, when he returns in the afternoon he has a suitable insert. With the insert in place, the saw works as well as it probably did when new and the replacement blade makes beautiful cuts. We are ready to finish the veranda.

Except that the heavily modified blade guard now throws out considerably more water than before and drenches whoever is cutting the tile. Liz duct–tapes a piece of heavy plastic along the side to extend the edge down to where it was before the butchery began, and the water again behaves itself. The new water skirt isn't pretty, but it works just fine.

We call this final improvement a *gringonada*. I can't wait to hear what Francis calls it.

***

3

A s the morning progressed, Robert reflected once again that he was lucky to be here, in this special place, after having traveled so much and seen so much of the world, and even seen more of Mexico than most of his Mexican neighbors. Few of them had ever traveled far from the village, and most had never been out of the state of Sonora. An exception was Zana, their stout muscular Mayan friend who came here from Mayab, his ancestral lands in Yucatán, about thirty years ago on his way to the US and never got any further. He was resourceful and made a good living as a *buceo*, a diver for lobsters, and as a cook for gringo hunting expeditions to the big island. And now he was part of the scene here in Tiburón. Tonight Robert and Liz would be hanging out at Zana's place with a bunch of friends for a *sarandeado*, a big fish dressed with a layer of chopped vegetables and Zana's special spices. And Robert would bring a fresh bottle of good tequila to share after dinner with Zana, who would once again spin his tales of adventure on the Sea. Which even included a stint of diving out there with Jacques Cousteau. At least according to Zana.

The last time at Zana's, Robert had a special bottle of bootleg *bacanora*—Sonora's local version of tequila—that he'd scored up in the Río Sonora Valley, in Banámichi. It came in a recycled J&B Scotch bottle with a cork in it, and it tasted good and smoky. But Zana and twelve good friends had drained it over the course of a lengthy evening, and it was a long trip back to Banámichi for a refill. So this time Robert would only pony up a decent tequila. And he fondly recalled the first time he ever got his hands on a precious bottle of *bacanora*, in the quiet little mountain town of Ures.

***

The Twice-Smuggled Bottle

Robert had never really meant to become a smuggler, especially at his age. But it just seemed to work out that way on this trip north to the border.

It was Liz who suggested they take a different route to the Arizona border this time. The hottest days of summer had descended on the Sonoran coast, as usual around the middle of July, so it seemed like as good a time as any to visit friends and family *en el otro lado,* on the other side, as Sonorans called the US.

They made their usual preparations for the trip and moved Juan and Lupita into their casa on the

beach again, like they had last year, and left them
in charge of things in case, say, a hurricane hit
while they were north. There are a lot of obstacles
to slow down a hurricane—like the entire
mountainous Baja Peninsula, for example—so
they rarely hit this part of the coast. Usually, they
hit Cabo or La Paz or even Guaymas, and left
Tiburón alone. Robert remembered standing on
the beach last year under a calm, overcast sky,
and watching one of those big grey monsters surge
up the Sea toward Tiburón, and then recede
before it moved inland over Guaymas and then
onward to quench the thirsty peaks and tall pine
forests of the Sierra Madre. It caused a lot of
damage in the Guaymas area and mangled
western Mexico's main coastal highway in three
places, but Tiburón escaped with no damage at
all, except for the rafts of debris that washed ashore
over the next week or so. Robert still had a large
cactus log that drifted ashore, and he put it under
the mesquite tree in the side yard as a reminder.

Most of the locals like to think the town's
patron saint protects them and sends the
hurricanes elsewhere. A few say there's just not
enough of interest in Tiburón for a decent
hurricane to bother with. If a hurricane's gonna go
to all that much trouble, it might as well nail the
wealthy enclaves over at Cabo. But by the time
one of these monster storms passes over the spine
of the Baja, those tall desert mountains have
usually dragged the wind speed down to tropical

depression status, and the Sonoran coast only gets drenched with unbelievable quantities of water. It's almost the only time each year that this part of the coast sees rainfall. It's the moment the towering and thirsty cardón cactus wait for all year.

Robert had his cellphone fully charged and Juan had the number to call in case anything went wrong, so Liz was feeling relaxed about the trip. Just north of Hermosillo she suggested they take the route into the mountains, through Ures, for a bit of variety. Ures was the old capital of Sonora.

Robert looked over at Liz. He was surprised at this sudden suggestion, even after all these years. It wasn't the first time Liz had suggested a sudden change to the planned itinerary, and he still always managed to look surprised. Sometimes he thought she actually did that just to see his reaction, to see if he still had any interest in adventures.

"What about a place to stay?" he asked, "Are there any hotels there? Do you know anything about the place?"

"Nope," Liz said, and smiled.

Robert looked at Liz again and then looked back at the road. The turnoff was just up ahead.

"I just think there has to be something interesting to see there," she continued. "I mean it's the old capital, isn't it? And there has to be some kind of hotel there."

"Well, I suppose so," Robert said, skeptically. "I guess we can always sleep in the van, if worse comes to worse."

"Worse" seemed to sum up the basic premise of Robert's world view. As in "What's the worst that can happen?" Robert tended to envision the worst, while Liz seemed to go through life expecting that only good things would happen. He eased over to the right side of the four-lane international highway and slowed for the Ures turnoff. It was a two-lane road that looked to be in decent enough condition. "So far, so good," he thought.

After passing through San Pedro El Saucito, a farming community in a small desert valley, the road headed into the foothills of the Sierra Madre Occidental. Small scrub juniper and piñon clung to the rocks. There was a simple beauty to the land, a hardscrabble land, like most of northern Mexico.

After about 45 minutes of driving they arrived at the outskirts of Ures where the road split and the right-hand lane became a one-way street through the back neighborhoods of the town, which were probably quiet and peaceful until they had to deal with this new wave of speeding traffic. Robert and Liz were the only ones on the road and he wondered why anyone had bothered to make it a one-way street. He mulled over the Mexican fascination with one-way streets, as if it were a distinctive mark of modernization. If you had one-way streets, you must be on the pathway to the future—the surest way to economic development. Cities in the US were now busily abandoning their one-way grids and trying to repair the damage all that unnecessary speeding traffic had done to their neighborhoods. But Mexico still worshiped them. Hermosillo was full of them. He speculated about the rush hour here in tiny Ures and shook his head. All this for maybe two or three trucks per hour. And soon Robert and Liz were leaving the city.

The two one-ways had reunited into a two-lane road leading off into the countryside. They had not passed anything that looked like a plaza, or the center of town. After driving for another kilometer or so, Robert pulled over onto a broad area of the shoulder where many others had done so before.

"I think we must have missed the center of town," he said. "Surely there's more to it than that. There have to be some old buildings somewhere, unless they tore them all down. That doesn't seem likely. Maybe it's on the other one-way."

He turned the car around and drove back into Ures, this time looking down side streets to see if the plaza was hidden somewhere.

"There it is!" Liz said, "Down that street back there. Turn right at this next corner."

Robert had already begun to turn right. They often had the same thought at the same time. It was weird, Robert thought, sometimes.

They drove about four blocks and came to a quiet little plaza with towering trees and a small church at the far end. Robert parked the car on the mostly deserted street and they stepped out to take a walk. A couple of kids came over and tried out their minimal English, saying, "How are you?" with a heavy accent.

Robert said, "I am fine. How are you?" and they giggled and fled the scene, having exhausted their supply of English.

The whole little town seemed ancient, and the streets they drove in on looked like a deserted movie set from about 1890. They crossed the street to look at one of the older buildings and then worked their way toward the church.

Then a large white sedan pulled up to the curb and a guy wearing a white cowboy hat leaned across his wife sitting in the front seat to ask, "Where you from?" It hadn't taken them long to realize that older gringos were probably in short supply around Ures and they would quickly be an object of curiosity.

Liz addressed him in Spanish, honed by her time in the Peace Corps, and the conversation became more animated. He had a restaurant just two blocks away and they needed to stop in there for a meal, he told them, because his wife was the best cook in town. They noted the location and thanked him for the invitation, but it was only mid morning and a bit too early for lunch. They assured him they would stop by later then went on to look at the old church.

It was a simple adobe church building, dating back to the 1600s or 1700s, and it was a nice spot to relax in one of the ancient wooden pews for a

few minutes to soak up the enduring quiet of an
old Mexican village. After a relaxing respite, they
wandered down a few more old dusty streets past
centuries of local history, as the sun began to
shorten the shadows until it finally stood high
overhead. The entire town was quiet and the
streets deserted, as people remained inside until
the cool of the evening. When the afternoon heat
increased, Robert and Liz angled back toward the
plaza and found the restaurant that belonged to
the guy in the white hat.

They stepped inside the thick cool adobe
walls, nodded to the young girl standing by the
kitchen door, and took a couple of plastic seats at
one of the small metal tables provided by Coca
Cola. The young girl had a look of panic in her
large brown eyes when they arrived, and she
quickly disappeared out the door and down the
sidewalk. After a few minutes, the guy who had
greeted them on the plaza came in, dragging his
wife with him, and with a guitar in the other hand.

He introduced himself as Avelino and helped
his wife take their order for cheese enchiladas and
two Coca Colas. Then he played a couple of
1950s US rock songs on the guitar, complete with
heavily-accented lyrics. His pronunciation was
almost comical, as if he really didn't speak much
English but knew mostly what the words should
sound like, and Robert and Liz did their best not
to laugh. After that intro, Robert asked if he knew
"Maquina 501," a song about the famous train

wreck at the mining town of Nacozari de Garcia back in 1907. They really didn't want to hear corny US rock oldies in the mountains of Sonora.

Avelino was surprised the gringo would even know about such an old bit of Sonoran folklore. He had grown up hearing his uncles sing that song, but it had been many years since he'd joined them around the campfire and he had to think for a moment about the words. Then he embarked on the tragic tale of Jesús Garcia, the revered train engineer who saved Nacozari from destruction.

Jesús stopped the train to see his mother but soon learned that a fire had broken out in the brakes on one of the cars carrying dynamite, so he climbed back into the cab and drove the train to a safe spot out of town where it exploded. He was killed by the explosion. They renamed the town after him, and a monument to Jesus Garcia and the historic event stands today on the plaza of Nacozari de Garcia.

After several more Mexican ballads, Avelino brought out an old J&B bottle filled with a colorless liquid. It was *bacanora,* the local home-brewed firewater version of tequila. A smoky-sweet smell of fire-roasted agave wafted from the bottle as he poured them each a shot into small glasses.

Liz sniffed the brew and said, "It smells like something you'd treat wounds with." Avelino missed her meaning, so she used the term "medicinal" instead. He agreed that it was *medicinal* and important to good health, and then he slammed his shot down the throat while his new gringo friends took small sips to savor the moment—and also to avoid damaging their innards. After Avelino poured a second round, which they dutifully enjoyed, they decided it would be a good idea to make an exit. And somehow in the process Robert managed to buy himself a full bottle of local bacanora before he got away. It came in a clear quart beer bottle with a Miller High Life screw-on cap.

"Are you gonna drink all that before we get to the border tomorrow?" Liz asked as they wandered carefully out the door. She often asked that sort of question.

"No. We'll smuggle it across the border in the ice chest and tell them it's a bottle of water. I want my cousin Eric, the wine snob, to get a snort of it. I wonder if he's ever had any bootleg liquor." A couple of shots of strong booze always seemed to give Robert those kinds of good ideas.

Liz glanced at Robert but let it go. When they got arrested at the border, she planned to tell them she knew nothing about it. It was all Robert's idea. And his problem.

Robert and Liz made their way to a simple old adobe inn near the plaza that Avelino had recommended. It had been a nice hacienda long ago but now needed a good scrub down, significant repair, and lots of paint. There was a small room available off the courtyard for only twenty dollars. The door lock was a cheap screen door hook and eye; but the mattress wasn't too lumpy and the sheets smelled clean, so they laid back for an afternoon siesta. In the evening they went back to the plaza for some tacos from a street vendor, and they watched as he carefully made up their order then covered his hands with two open plastic bags he kept beside his worktable before he took their money and made their change. It was a reminder that the filthiest stuff that most people ever touch is probably the money in their own pockets.

They wandered the plaza enjoying their tacos in the cool evening air and wished it were a weekend so the local band might be playing old tunes in the bandstand for the *viejitos* who spend those evenings in the plaza, just as their ancestors had done over the past several centuries. Then they settled onto an old wrought iron park bench with a couple of ice cream bars to watch the traditional evening life of a small Mexican village unfold, as it had for so many generations before they arrived. Some young boys had a pickup *fútbol* game going at one end of the plaza, and a boom box by the ice vendor was playing Mexican ballads. The tranquility and timelessness of this place was so beguiling that they thought for a moment it might be a wonderful place to resettle. It was a romantic and ridiculous idea, of course, because they would never be fully accepted into this tight-knit little community in the sierra. But Robert and Liz often enjoyed entertaining romantic and ridiculous ideas.

In the quiet morning they bid farewell to Ures and headed north on the wide dirt road that would take them to Rayón. It was easy driving—easier than they had hoped, as the road had been re-bladed recently and the terrain was mostly flat. It also appeared to be a kind of short cut back to the main highway instead of continuing up the Rio Sonora Valley. In the distance the knife-edged peaks of the sierra sliced across a crystalline desert sky. About half an hour into the trip they came to a series of easy dips as the road crossed several dry washes. But Robert took one of them a bit too fast and he heard a crunch as the oil pan bottomed onto an exposed rock. He stopped the van at the top of the next rise and put it into reverse.

"What's wrong?" Liz asked.

"Just checking," he replied.

As he backed the van down, a pair of oily trails appeared on the clean dirt road. Then he put the van back into forward gear and hoped they weren't too far from Rayón.

He was more careful in the dips after that mishap, although it was probably irrelevant now. After topping a couple more rises, they came to a traffic gate lowered across the road. Out in the middle of nowhere. A guy rose from an old plastic chair and wandered over to the car to explain they were just raising money for Rayón's upcoming fiesta. Robert was relieved that they'd arrived in Rayón and quickly handed him a 100-peso bill donation, while Liz asked if there was *un mecánico* in town. The guy seemed shocked at the large bill and quickly raised the gate, while saying the *mecánico* was *"muy cerquita, a la izquierda de la carretera."*

Robert soon turned left at a crude *"mecánico"* sign scrawled on a broken piece of plywood, and quickly shut off the engine as a very large fellow rose from a rusty metal chair under a shade tree. There was no actual repair garage in sight. Just the shade tree, and the mechanic who had been sitting there with his mother. His surprised expression said that he hadn't expected to see any gringos pull up to his casa lately. He introduced himself as José while Liz explained their situation, then he knelt in the dirt to look under the car.

When Robert heard him say, "Uh oh," he knew he had a problem.

José used a decrepit-looking jack to lift the car and he put an oil-stained concrete block under it as a support. Then he shimmied under the car with a few tools to remove the oil pan. He showed Robert the ugly gouges and bent metal from the rock impact and the torn gasket that looked like it couldn't be saved, and Robert wondered how many days they'd be stuck in Rayón waiting for parts to arrive. He doubted there was a hotel of any sort in a town this small, or any good place to eat. Then José calmly gestured to his truck, indicating that the two of them would go get the mangled oil pan repaired.

Meanwhile, Liz sat under the shade tree with José's mom, and they had a fine long conversation in Spanish about their families and friends, and the upcoming village fiesta.

José pulled up to a welding shop that was owned by a friend of his and they discussed how to fix the oil pan, while Robert tried to follow the conversation. The welder put the oil pan into a vise and got out a big hammer. In just a few very loud minutes the bent metal was straightened and then braised back together, and Robert reached for some money to pay the welder. He was out in the middle of nowhere with no other choices, and he hoped they'd go easy on him. Then the welder smiled broadly and said, "The *mecánico,* he my friend. I fix it for him." There would be no charge. Robert gave a surprised laugh and shook the welder's hand in gratitude.

Then they were off to a small auto parts shop to pick up several quarts of oil and a couple of tubes of silicone caulk for making a gasket, before heading back to the car. After a short time, the oil pan was reinstalled and Robert started the engine to check for leaks. Everything was back in order and Robert asked how much he owed. José sheepishly replied, *"Doscientos pesos."*

All that hassle, and he only wanted 20 bucks? Robert thanked him as he forked over 250 pesos. He considered paying more but held it at 25 bucks so the guy wouldn't be offended by getting too much money after helping his new friend. Robert knew again that this sort of thing was one of the many reasons he really liked living and traveling in Mexico. The people in these old mountain villages were a special breed, indeed.

At the small plaza in Rayón, they took the direct paved route back to the main highway and wound their way through cactus-covered desert hills, passing a small herd of burros on the way. And Liz filled him in on the nice conversation she'd had with José's mom. It seems she wanted them to spend the night at her house so they could attend the village fiesta, which is one of the big events of the year. And all the rest of the way to the border Robert couldn't wipe the smile off his face just thinking about the wonderful generosity of these mountain folks.

It was late when Robert and Liz reached the Naco border crossing. The guard looked exhausted after a long day, so he took a quick glance at the two harmless-looking old gringos and their mostly-empty van, and waved them through. All they had to worry about now was getting that prized bottle of *bacanora* back into Mexico when they returned in a month or two— if there was any left by then.

As Robert recalled this tale he remembered one of the old-timers who said long ago, "If you're gonna live down here, you'll learn to become a good smuggler."

Robert and Liz would return to Ures several times over the years, and one time they brought their friends Kath and Phil, who had a blues band in DC. On this occasion they had a fine luncheon in Avelino's ancient family casa on a corner of the plaza as he again played Sonoran folksongs on the guitar. When Robert mentioned that Kate and Phil played blues tunes, Avelino passed the guitar to Kate, and she performed a few numbers while Phil pulled out his blues harp to accompany her. Avelino grabbed his video recorder to get some footage of the event. When Robert mentioned that Kate also played *teclado* (keyboards), Avelino's eyebrows rose and he motioned everyone to follow him to the front corner room that looked onto the plaza and the church. He opened the door to show them a Steinway piano that his grandfather had ordered long ago from San Francisco. When it arrived on a steamship in Guaymas his grandfather and a couple of strong workers had gone down to the dock with an old truck and hauled it over rough dirt roads into the mountains as a prized possession.

Avelino whipped out the video recorder again as Kate played the well-worn old ivory keys, and she leaned back just a bit so he could get the left hand action that's essential to the blues. And as they left, Robert managed to score another bottle of the best local *bacanora* to take back to the beach.

***

As Robert reflected on those many fine past visits to a little village in the Sierra, he watched a couple of fishermen in a panga returning from the islands with their daily catch. It looked like Juan and his cousin Tomás, but his binoculars were inside on the kitchen table and he couldn't be sure due to the distance. The quotidian life of Tiburón went on uninterrupted, as it had for years now.

He settled back into his beach chair and reflected on the pathway that led him here. And he reflected on the fact that he was actually reflecting at all—that reflection is for the old and that he wasn't really all that old. Not yet anyway. Not like some sad J. Alfred Prufrock bemoaning the tattered remnants of a life never truly lived.

"Let us go then, you and I, when the evening spreads out across the sky, like a patient etherized upon a table."

At least that's how he remembered the poem; it had been a while since he'd read it. Robert encountered those opening lines of TS Eliot's classic poem when he was a college sophomore who had recently switched from a major in philosophy to the equally impractical study of English literature.

It was a potent image when Robert was young—a portent of an old age that he would maybe reach some day in the distant future. An age when he would also *"… wear white flannel trousers and walk upon the beach."* And now he smiled at his baggy tan nylon hiking shorts with bulging pockets, the ones he wore each day, and the cotton T-shirt he'd plucked from the pile in his closet. He made a lot of mistakes in life but had somehow attained *la*

tercera edad—the third age, as they call it in Mexico—
and the current fashions were a lot different than old Eliot
could have imagined. He might have cringed at the way
people dress today, including aging gringo retirees
slouched on Mexican verandas overlooking the beach.

4

The common image of drunken gringos living out their dissipated lives on a Mexican beach didn't really apply all that much to Tiburón, as most of the local expats led a healthy and active lifestyle that included lots of early morning wake-ups for fishing trips in the Sea of Cortez. But the thing that surprised Robert most about retiring to a small beach town was the way it pried him out of the comfortable intellectual bubble he inhabited for so many years back in Albuquerque. He'd been content to live that way, as it provided plenty of mental fodder to keep the mind active. But this new environment had put him into contact—direct daily contact—with a wide variety of people whose ideas were contrary to his own. And he found there was also a wider stretch of common ground than he had imagined. Some of the richest and most right-wing characters in town were the first to pitch in a hundred dollar bill to help out a local family that was left destitute after a fire or similar tragedy, and with the comment, "Just don't say where it came from." And it wasn't that they did not want to be associated with the effort; they just didn't want the credit for it. They just wanted to help out.

Robert realized that the kind of people who settle in Tiburón were an eclectic bunch with interesting back stories. They were actually willing to cross the border into Mexico, and that alone set them off from most of the U.S. population. They avoided the usual tourist traps to find themselves here in a small town at the end of a narrow road, and they were willing to deal with all the vagaries and challenges of a very different culture. They were end-of-the-road people, and that also had to say something in their favor.

***

Pemex and Dr Jim

Dr Jim was fed up. He'd been cheated for the last time by Eduardo, the manager of the local Pemex station, the only gas station in town, the local monopoly. Dr Jim had just returned from a long day in the desert with Clyde, his plant biologist buddy, where they found a few stone arrowheads among the dry wind-chiseled mountains, and Clyde showed him the largest cardón cactus he knew of in this part of Sonora. There was a picture of this towering multi-armed specimen in the book that Clyde had published recently about the rich variety of hardy local plants clustered in this area, but he didn't generally let people know where it was. Today's trip with Clyde made Dr Jim feel like a privileged member of a secret society.

And now the gas tank on the old dust-covered Nissan SUV was reading empty. Eva, the girl at the pump, put almost 100 liters into the tank. But Dr Jim knew the tank capacity was only somewhere around 70 or 80 liters, according to the Owner's Manual in the glove compartment. He pointed this out to Eva in his halting Spanish.

He knew Eva and her family. It was hard not to know just about everybody in the isolated little town of Tiburón. They lived in a half-finished shack with a dirt floor and no windows, but the two young boys always had clean uniforms and backpacks for school. Her husband Raúl was a fisherman. He spent most days out on the Sea of Cortez in a panga, in the blazing sun of summer and the cold winds of winter. And he'd spent more than a few cold nights diving for lobster, using the risky equipment and that unfiltered air compressor the dive boat owner provided. He knew that the oily air he was breathing was wrecking his lungs, but he needed the work. It was a hard life.

Eva didn't understand much of Dr Jim's halting Spanish about the gas tank capacity on a Nissan SUV, but he didn't sound happy. And she didn't know what to say to the nice gringo Doctor who had cared for her and her children at the clinic, and had never charged them for it. She smiled weakly and pointed at the pump readout.

It was generally understood in the backwater town of Tiburón, and throughout most of Mexico, that the gas mileage your car got on the highway was directly related to the Pemex station where you'd last filled up. It could vary widely, depending on how much each dealer rigged his pumps. It was really meaningless to check your mileage, and there was no recourse. You had just one choice—to pay up and pour yourself a cold margarita when you got home, to be thankful for the sweeping view from your veranda of the Sea of Cortez, and to enjoy your time in this wonderful but challenging country. That's just the way things are sometimes.

Dr Jim loved the winter seasons he spent in Mexico, in this little town with its wonderful people. And he was often amused by the quirky culture he lived in. Most of the time he wasn't much bothered by the power outages and the many potholes that kept this place from becoming another tourist magnet. He actually thought most of that was a good thing. And the public events that always began at least an hour after the posted time. He was living on Mexican Time these days, and he accepted that. He also liked being far away from the toxic US political climate these days. Sure it was a copout, but he slept better not being faced with it constantly. Down here he could only be an amused observer of Mexican politics, as the country endlessly continued to fumble its way through a semi-workable democracy.

But every time he forked over the money registered on the pump it galled him that the gas pumps were so blatantly dishonest. He handed Eva several large peso notes, and while he remembered that she spoke no English, he grumbled about it again anyway. To nobody in particular. But this time he decided that on his next trip north of the border he'd find one of those official buckets they use in Arizona to check the calibration of the gas pumps. Then he'd be ready to deal with the Pemex issue. Right after he took care of all the other things that always seem to dominate a person's daily life.

Then his phone rang. As a semi-retired ER Doc, Jim was always on call in this expat community of US and Canadian winter refugees. And he actually enjoyed the involvement with his community. He enjoyed being needed. People would call about the oddest things, and Dr Jim would do his best to patch them up, or calm them down. Maybe hold their hands for a moment or two. Like with Claire, from Calgary, and her panic attacks.

It was still early in The Season and there were none of the usual retired paramedics or other First Responders in town who usually dealt with it. So Dr Jim showed up at her door, yet again, with his little black doctor bag in hand, just like in an old movie. It was a point of pride for him that he could deal with most health problems without computers and those other modern tools that often seemed to give back false information. And his old well-traveled little black bag was amusingly reassuring for his patients.

Soon Claire was settled and able to cope with the day. She was not having a heart attack. She'd never had a heart attack yet, but it was a constant worry. She probably read too many self-medication stories on the internet and should find another way to pass the time of day. A few of Dr Jim's retired expat patients seemed to have a similar addiction to the internet. That, or drinking too much.

There was a knock on the door just after he got home, and this time it was Earl, who came in from fishing with a lure stuck in his ear.

"With all the fish that are living out there in the Sea of Cortez," Earl explained, "my fishing buddy Harold managed to catch me. Right in the ear."

It was a simple patch-up job, after cutting off the hook barb, and it would be worth more than a few good stories at Happy Hour at the Club. Dr Jim looked forward to the next time he'd be out fishing with Earl. It was always an interesting experience, and Earl knew where the fish were. He was one of those guys who could see the X on the water that was invisible to mere mortals like the rest of us—the X that said, "Drop your hook right here."

Then there was the call from Joyce, a retired
graphic designer from New Mexico who never
called the doctor. When he heard her voice,
Dr Jim knew it had to be something important.
Joyce was in excruciating pain and writhing on
the floor of her house. She hadn't wanted to call
but her husband George was away at a mid-
morning Spanish lesson where the phone was off
the hook, and she didn't know what else to do.

"I'm going to ask you three questions," Dr Jim
said into the phone. "First, where is the pain?"

Joyce answered, "It's in my lower left side,
near the groin."

"Describe the pain."

"It feels like someone has stuck a knife into
me and is twisting it."

"I'll be right over."

Joyce was passing a kidney stone, and the
pain was intense as the needle-edged particle
sliced its way through the narrow passages of the
urinary tract. A shot of Demerol soon put her
into a giddy trip-like state and the stone passed.
It was the most intense pain she'd ever had, but
it ended quickly. When George returned after his
class, he found Joyce half asleep and blissfully
incoherent. She never did know what Dr Jim's
third question might have been, but she saved
the stone so the local lab could analyze it and
Dr Jim could suggest a dietary change or two.

But Dr Jim was still very much concerned
about those gas pumps and about that gas

bucket that he intended to bring back to
Tiburón. So after a Thanksgiving trip north to
visit his sister in Oregon, Dr Jim returned to
Tiburón with an official-looking gas measuring
bucket. When he'd finished with his last
patients for the day, he set the bucket onto the
passenger side floor of his Nissan SUV and
drove to the Pemex station. Eduardo the owner
was there taking care of various tasks, and he
made a point of ignoring the complaining
gringo. Dr Jim set his official bucket on the
concrete by the pump and told Eva to fill it to
the 1-liter line. She listened to his fumbled
Spanish and looked puzzled at the bucket.
"*Aqui,*" he said, and pointed at the line.

Eduardo glanced over from the large Coke
machine that he was refilling with the world's
best-selling sugar water, which was probably the
main source of Mexico's obesity crisis. So many
Mexican families seemed to start their kids out
each morning with a huge liter bottle of Coke.
That was another thing that Dr Jim wanted to
deal with in some way, but he didn't know how.
That would happen sometime later. Right now he
was focused on the Pemex issue.

Eva looked at Dr Jim as she put the pump
hose nozzle into the bucket. "*Si,*" he nodded.
"Up to *aqui.*" And he pointed again to the 1-liter
line. Eva filled it just to the line and stopped the
pump. They both looked at the pump, which
read 1.25 liters, and showed the price.

Dr Jim pointed at the pump readout, triumphantly lifted the official bucket, and marched over to Eduardo as Eva stood holding the hose.

"You see this?" he demanded.

Eduardo glanced at the evidence in the bucket.

"I've been telling you your pumps are crooked for at least a year now," said Dr Jim.

Eduardo replied in the refined English he'd learned long ago in one of the better prep schools of Hermosillo. "Of course, my friend."

Dr Jim stared at Eduardo and his unflappable demeanor in the face of incontrovertible proof.

"The guy who delivers the gas screws me," Eduardo continued in his well-modulated voice, "so I have to screw you. Hey, nice bucket."

Later that evening Dr Jim was sitting in his living room with a glass of good Mexican brandy and restlessly reading the latest issue of JAMA. But mostly he was still distracted by the gas station drama, and he set the Journal aside to stare at the Sea rolling endlessly to the shore. It was a boring article anyway, like most of those medical reports he was supposed to keep up with.

Then he burst out laughing as he recalled his friend Robert once saying, "If you don't have a perverse sense of humor you may not do well living here in Mexico."

So he was going to do what, exactly, with his stupid US-certified gas measuring bucket? Change Mexico? Nobody down here really gave a damn anyway. Or at least they realized there was nothing they could do to change it. He could imagine Eduardo thinking, "So I still gotta explain everything here to you gringos?"

Dr Jim took another swallow of brandy, shook his head, and smiled as his gaze shifted to the large rock sitting on his seaside veranda that Dave, a college radical buddy of his, had wrestled up from the beach. A seagull was standing on it waiting for a handout. Dr Jim had spent his college days studying in classrooms and labs, or locked in the library, while Dave spent his days on protest picket lines and his nights wrapped in marijuana and wine. And they had both become successful doctors. Go figure.

He stared beyond Dave's Rock into a cloudless sky as the last rays of a fading sun cast bands of fiery rubies across the wave tops of the broad Sea of Cortez. He could just make out those distant desert headlands on the far side, over there on the Baja Peninsula, and he still planned to visit them again someday, with his old buddy Clyde.

***

Fabiola

Everybody in Bahía Tiburón seemed to notice when Fabiola came to town, although it was hard to figure whether it was the women or the men who noticed her first. She was strikingly good-looking, a bit younger than most of the retired expat women in town, certainly too young to be retired in the usual sense of the word, and everybody seemed to take an interest in her. The word on the street was that she was single, which seemed to generate a mostly negative interest on the part of the women. And among the men, the level of interest was something approaching the fascinated fear that a man might feel at the brink of a precipice where the mind is saying, "Crawl slowly back from the edge," while some primal bodily urge is screaming "Go ahead and jump! This could be your last chance ever to feel the exhilaration of living your life to the fullest!"

"Flabiola" is what the women would have liked to call her, so they could cut her to the bone with a simple nickname, but they really couldn't call her that since she ran about five miles almost every morning on the beach, there wasn't a bit of flab on her, and she resembled a gazelle more than she resembled any of the other women in town. So "Fabulosa" was the name a few of the women branded her with. The word was that Fabiola was half-Mexican and half-American, whatever that meant, since the Mexicans also considered themselves as part of the Americas. Ruth Cosgrove came from Iowa farm stock, and she said the name and everything else about her was "pure made up," in the way they say things like that on farms in Iowa so that it comes out sounding like the honest-to-God truth. The truth is, Ruth didn't really know any more about Fabiola than the other women, but that's what they were all thinking; and she said it first, so it stuck as one of those truths that live forever in small towns and are the reason many people move away when they graduate from high school.

Fred Carson was one of the first of the men to notice Fabiola. He was a widower with a decent pension and enough money in the bank and in his IRA to pretty much do what he wanted for the rest of his life, as long as he didn't waste it. He had a nice-looking house on the beach, although it wasn't exactly a mansion, and a older model 28-foot fishing boat that he could take out to the islands for an overnighter whenever he wanted to. He also tried to get down to the local Gringo Club, as the Mexicans called it, for morning walking aerobics three times a week, when he wasn't out fishing, so he wouldn't be tempted to stay around in the house by himself for more hours than he should. He was determined to stay in good enough shape to get the most out of his retirement years, and he enjoyed the company of his fellow exercisers. The majority of retirees in Tiburón did what they could to stay in semi-decent shape and make the most out of their final years.

The morning sessions at the Club were also part of the informal Tiburón Telegraph, where people passed on bits of information—call it gossip, if you have to—about the weather, other residents, changes in Mexican regulations, etc. They also shared tips about how to find Pancho the electrician, or Nacho the plumber, when you needed them, since neither one had a phone and they were usually working somewhere around town. The walking aerobics and the Club's Friday night Social Hour helped Fred stay in touch with his fellow expats.

He had seen Fabiola run past his place a few times while he was dressing for aerobics, and he usually reached for his binoculars to watch her as she went by. Sometimes she would stop running and walk about a mile before running again. She looked to be in her late 40s to early 50s, as best he could tell from a distance. Fred had heard that phrase, "There's no fool like an old fool," and she was at least ten years younger than he was. He knew that's what most of the women in town were thinking, especially a few of the single ones who'd invited him to dinner a time or two. He knew that many of the married women saw Fabiola as a temptation to their husbands, and the widows saw her as unwelcome and unfair competition for the few desirable men in town. But Fred hadn't met anyone else who interested him as a partner in the four years he'd lived in Tiburón.

As he stood there by the window looking down the beach at Fabiola receding into the distance, Fred thought to himself, "I only just started collecting Social Security, so I'm really not all that old. I'm a long ways from dead, yet." And, "If not now, then when?" He also thought, "The hell with what those old biddies think!"

One Tuesday morning he walked down to the water's edge and tried to appear like he was studying the weather. He looked up to watch her race by and he just had time to say, "Hello."

She half turned and said "Hi" over her shoulder as she ran onward on the flat hard sand margin along the waterline. He watched her race away for just a little longer than was probably decent as he admired the way her loose jogging shorts hugged her nicely-rounded body. Then he caught himself and looked away before any of the neighbors saw him staring. The whole beach was wide open and many people began their day with coffee and looking out at the water, or going for long walks along the water's edge. He hoped he wouldn't already be food for the gossip mill, but he knew that was probably inevitable in this town.

Velma Parsons took a sip of her margarita and studied her cards. She was one of the regulars at the Tiburón Ladies Liquor League that met for cards, drinks, and a bite of lunch at Jose's Restaurante y Bar every Wednesday. It gave her something to do after her husband Bart passed away. The Ladies' weekly "May I" game helped to keep her sharp. She looked up just as Carol Birch discarded.

"I'll take that one," she said.

"You're supposed to say 'May I?'" said Rita Johnson.

"Oh, don't be so formal," Velma replied, "Anybody else want it?"

Glenda Thompson, the fourth player at the table, shook her head, so Velma pushed one of her chips to the center, pulled that fresh seven off the top of the pile and drew two more cards. Now she had a group of sevens, a pair of eights, and a bunch of junk in her hand that she still couldn't figure out what to do with. She took another sip off the margarita while Rita drew a card.

"Did anybody else see Fred almost throw his neck out of joint yesterday when Fabiola ran by?" Velma pretended to be studying her cards as she tossed this zinger out to the other players. She was Fred's next door neighbor and had been enjoying her usual morning coffee looking out at the ocean when she saw him appear on the beach. She'd thought it odd when he walked toward the water, since he was rarely seen on that side of his house. When he wasn't out fishing, he was usually on the street side working on his car, or inside checking the internet weather on his computer.

The other three pairs of eyes at the table looked up briefly, and then went back to silently studying their cards. None of them wanted to appear too curious, but all ears were now tuned toward Velma.

"Well, it looked like he said something to her, but she just blew on past him. He stood there staring after her for a while and I think I even saw him drooling."

"A lot of men at his age drool," said Carol. "And they're incontinent, too!"

"Are you talking about Joe?" asked Rita, referring to Carol's husband.

"Exactly!" said Carol.

"No really, from the look on Fred's face you'd think he was afraid he forgot where he stashed his Viagra." Velma pressed on, returning the conversation to where she'd started it.

"Oh, come on," Glenda chuckled.

"No, really. Then he turned around to see if anybody was watching him. He looked like a guilty little kid caught with his hand in the cookie jar."

"Or someplace else, maybe," added Carol.

They laughed, and Glenda said, "Maybe this is why they call us the Beach Bitches."

"Yeah, probably," said Rita as she discarded. "I'll take that card," said Glenda.

The next few days were windy and not good for fishing, and Fred stayed inside his house so he wouldn't look too obvious. But then, on Saturday morning, he saw Fabiola standing at the water's edge watching flocks of squawking pelicans, terns, and gulls diving into the water. From his porch, he could see the dark school of small fish that stretched for about a hundred yards in the water just off the beach. She was surprised when he appeared beside her and said "Hi."

"Oh, hi," she said, and glanced in his direction, "What's going on? What are the birds doing?"

"That's a 'bird pile,'" he said. "They're diving on that school of small fish you can see there in the water. It's that dark mass just below the surface."

"Really?" she said. "That just looks like the shadow of a cloud."

"Yes it does," Fred replied, "but there isn't a cloud in the sky."

Fabiola looked up into the piercingly blue and empty Sonoran sky, and then studied the water where the birds were crashing headlong, dozens at a time, into the surface. The excited squawking of a couple of hundred birds drowned out almost every other sound. It was difficult to understand why they didn't break their necks crashing into each other. Probably some did, now and then.

"We look for bird piles when we take the boat out fishing," said Fred. "Wherever there's a large school of small fish, it usually means there are big fish below. See that flash of silvery little fish over there leaping out of the water? There's a big fish underneath feeding on them from the bottom and they break the surface trying to escape. They're the basis of the food chain here in the Sea of Cortez. The big fish attack them from below and the birds get them from the top. Life's rough here if you're a little fish."

"You have a boat?" asked Fabiola.

"He took her out on his boat," said Velma, as she arranged her cards.

"Who took who out on his boat?" asked Brandy Hansen.

She was a new girl at the table this week, just in from Calgary, Alberta. In Canada. Velma wasn't looking forward to going through all the rules again. She'd also have to fill in all the background on that story too, so she sighed and looked a bit exasperated. Brandy looked startled as if she'd already said something wrong.

"Oh, don't worry about Velma," said Carol. She's always glad to have a new audience. And anyway, you'll catch up soon enough."

"Harvey said he saw them at the boat ramp on Sunday," Velma continued. "They went out to the big island. He said they didn't catch much of anything."

"You mean he didn't catch nothin'," said Carol. "That's what Harvey actually said. He doesn't think they actually planned to do much fishing out there in the first place. But it sounds like she's caught herself a big one."

"Yeah," added Glenda, "Looks like that trap she laid worked."

"What trap?" asked Brandy. This was sounding too juicy to fall very far behind on.

"That phony running on the beach in the skimpy jogging shorts," said Carol, adding, "Anybody want that card?"

"Yeah," said Velma, "I'll take it."

"Why you little vixen. That's the one I needed!" said Carol, as she waited her turn to draw.

"Too bad," said Velma. "Today's just my day. I can feel it already."

"So what are the odds on them showing up at the Club together for Happy Hour on Friday?" asked Glenda.

"Probably pretty good," said Carol. "If they can stay out of bed that long."

"Sounds like something I could use a little of," said Brandy.

The other three heads swiveled to study the new girl.

"Sounds like you're gonna fit in just fine around here," said Velma as she turned back to study her cards.

"How do you play this game, anyway?" asked Brandy, with a puzzled look.

It had been years since Fabiola had been back to Tiburón. She sat gazing out the window of her

rented beach house and remembered her first
visit to the Sea when her *abuelos* brought her to
the ocean from their village in a mountain valley
near Banámichi. She was born in the Sierra and
raised by her grandparents' in their old adobe
casa. It had been in the family for generations.
She had learned to feed the chickens and tend
the garden, and she knew where her food came
from. She even remembered the day when she
went to a *tienda* in town for the first time. There
was so much food on shelves along the walls.
Things she had never seen before.

Now she sat and watched the clean crystal
clarity of the green-tinted waves as they curled
and fell onto the beach, and she remembered
seeing them for the first time. They looked like
jewels, frozen for a moment in mid fall before
bursting into shards of glass that scattered the light
and foamed onto the sand. She was glad she had
returned. It just felt simple. It just felt right.

For the next three months there wasn't much
seen of Fred and Fabiola in Bahía Tiburón. At
least not in the usual places, like the Club. Some
of the guys who go in to Hermosillo every
Wednesday to play golf at the fancy Resort *Las
Palmas*, said they saw them on the course, and
afterward at the resort's pricey restaurant. Others
said they made several shopping trips to Tucson.
And Frank Wilson, who works in Hermosillo
running one of the *maquiladores,* said he saw

them at Los Toros Steak House, where the wealthy of Hermosillo are often seen.

"How would Fred even know about Los Toros?" asked Carol. "Must have been her idea. I heard she cut a broad swath through Hermosillo before she settled here. Damn, I sure needed that card you just took."

"Too bad," said Velma. "You weren't quick enough."

"No, but she sure was," said Glenda. "Fabiola, I mean."

"Yeah, we saw them here in town at the Blue Marlin the other night," said Carol. "And she looked like she'd just scored the Trifecta."

"You actually saw them?" said Velma. "They sure seem to find ways to use up their time. Well, if you're just gonna let that card sit there, I'll take it."

"Oh, damn," said Carol. "I need to pay more attention to this game."

"Harvey said that Fred seemed to spend lots of time nuzzled up to her on the golf course, helping her get her strokes right," said Rita.

"Oh, I don't think she needs any help getting her strokes right!" laughed Velma. "I think she probably does just fine in that department."

"And with all that running, she manages to keep the playground equipment in good shape," said Rita. "That's why all the guys are so happy to see her. They like to sneak a peak at the possibilities."

"Yeah," added Carol. "There's a lot of wishful thinking goes on in this town. As if any of the rest of them had a chance!"

"I think she's part Cherokee," said Velma. "There's lots of them back in Oklahoma. That's where she gets her exotic looks." Velma always said that about any woman who had exotic looks.

"Who's turn is it?" asked Brandy.

People hadn't seen much of Fred Carson at the local Gringo Club lately. He and Fabiola had taken a long trip, and spent a couple of months across the border, so the regulars were surprised to see him show up at Friday's Social Hour. He was alone. Don "Harley" Jackson was leaning on the bar waiting for a gin and tonic when Fred appeared beside him and ordered a Tecate, in a bottle.

"Haven't seen you in a while," Harley said. "Where's Fabiola?"

"She's visiting her mother in La Paz for a few days," answered Fred. "She's thinking things over."

"Uh oh," said Harley. "Thinking things over?"

"Yeah, things started moving a little too fast. She just needed some time to slow down."

"Oh," said Harley. He figured he better just let Fred talk. If he wanted to.

Fred took a big sip off the cold bottle. "Yeah, she ran into a guy with a bigger one. Boat, that is. You remember that 80-footer that was anchored out here a couple of weeks ago? That's the guy. He keeps the boat at Cabo and flies down from Phoenix to use it. Got more money than all us put together. It's hard to compete with that."

"Yeah, our thirty-year-old 25- to 30-footers look a little musty up beside that kind of shiny Gold-Plater," said Harley. "Sorry to hear it."

"Yeah," sighed Fred.

Harley continued, "The girls was saying over cards the other day they thought she'd been mixed up with that drug guy down in Sinaloa. The one in the papers about a month ago. The dead guy."

"She didn't talk a lot about that, but she seemed pretty shaken by the news," said Fred. "I couldn't tell whether he was her ex-husband, the abusive one she talked about, or maybe a relative. That's why we took that long trip up the West Coast. I wanted to get her mind off of it and show her some things she hadn't seen before."

"I bet you did," said Harley, with a grin. He took a long sip off his drink.

"Oh no!" said Fred. "She saw that long before we left. I meant a few of the museums around LA, the Bay Area, the Redwoods, and picking raspberries by the roadside in Oregon. That kind of stuff. She really liked the art museums, and picking those raspberries, while we watched out for bears. She's a country girl at heart."

"Did you go to Vegas?"

"No, we avoided Vegas. Her ex-husband took her there a few times, and she said she never wanted to go back. Said it was an empty place. No values. No meaning," said Fred. "I have to consider that a mark of character."

Fred decided to continue. "Look Harley, overall, I had a good run. With a fifteen-year age difference for starters, I didn't really think it would last. As I got to know her, I realized she was coming out of a real bad spot, and I just tried to be decent to her. We had a great time together, and she's a really great lady. I didn't come out one bit smarter, and I don't regret any of it."

Harley nodded and studied his drink.

Fred took a long sip on his beer. "When you gonna replace that Born To Be Wild tattoo on your arm with something more age-appropriate?"

"Like what?" Harley asked with a sidelong glance. "You mean something more like, 'Born To Be On Medicare?'"

Harley laughed at his own joke. "Yeah, the wild days are gone. I can't hardly walk anymore without this cane. Did you ever think it would come to this? A bunch of old guys on Medicare still trying to live out their fantasies on a beach in Mexico, and wishing we'd gotten here a lot sooner? I thought we were gonna be forever young, just like in that song."

"I feel your pain, Harley. I have to go back up to the VA every three months for more heart medicine," added Fred. "Say, what's the weather report for tomorrow?"

"Seas are flat, the water's warm, and the dorado are biting."

"I'll see you at the boat ramp early," said Fred as he finished his beer and turned to leave. "It's good to be back."

"I'll see you there," said Harley.

Mid-afternoon a month later, Fred was home after another good morning of fishing. It was Fall now and the water had cooled enough that the dorado had left, but there were a lot of hungry yellowtail out there now, and they were good fish, worth going after. He pulled a cold Tecate from the fridge and stepped out onto the veranda to look across the placid Sea of Cortez glistening beautiful and mysterious in the brilliant Sonoran sunlight. He knew the Sea would always be a mystery to him, in all her boisterous moods, a wilderness just below that shining surface, and that seemed to make life worthwhile. There was just a bit of the Baja visible way out there, now that it was a bit cooler and the air was drier with less sea haze hanging above the water.

Fred really liked that about the Fall and Winter here, when the temperature dropped and you could turn off the air-conditioner, leave the door open, and just listen to the Sea. It felt more meaningful than most of the babble of life. And in the Winter you could look all the way across the Sea to those distant headlands on the Baja, and the islands out there stood in such crisp bold relief it was hard to believe they were so far away. He leaned on the railing, took a long cold sip from the bottle, and reflected on how good life had been to him and how lucky he was to have a decent pension that would allow all this. Then the phone rang.

"Fred, it's Fabiola." The voice was tentative. "Can we talk?"

***

All his recollections reminded Robert of *I Remember Mama*, a TV show from the 1950s, where Mama, a kindly Swedish grandmother, *Sveedish* to the max, would come in to offer homespun wisdoms and sage advice to solve a difficult situation by the end of the show. It resonated with the post-war immigrant country that made up the U.S.— at least the Protestant Northern European immigrant population who replaced the native cultures who originally lived on the land.

But the people of Catholic Southern European origin who long ago settled in the southwestern US, and long before it became Mexico, were from a different culture. And the Mexican-American War was really about Protestant Northern Europeans against Catholic Southern Europeans. That's not how the textbooks in high school U.S. History class portrayed it, and it was much later when Robert learned more about the Mexican side of the story. Especially about the *San Patricios*, or Saint Patricks—

immigrants from Ireland to the US in the early 1820s who refused to fight against their Catholic brethren and went over to the Mexican side. And whenever they were captured by US troops they were tortured as traitors and murdered.

Robert became aware of this convoluted history when he began reading deeply into Mexican history in an effort to better understand the new country that he and Liz had decided to settle in. And so that he could have informed conversations with Mexican friends and workers, although most of them had little knowledge, or even interest, in their country's history, like the people he left behind in the US. Most people he met in life just seemed to live in the moment and had very little deep curiosity about how they and their family actually ended up living where they did.

Historians often debate whether human history follows any sort of logical narrative arc, or if it's just "one damn thing after another." And in the long run, what difference does it make anyway?

***

Karen

It seemed that Karen was never really capable of following anyone's good advice, of doing things by the book, and that's why she found herself in her later years living in a small Mexican beach town at the end of the road. She actually tried to escape a time or two, but always seemed to end up back in Bahía Tiburón with a lot of other odd,

end-of-the-road people who made her feel
comfortably at home. They weren't exactly all
societal rejects, although some were, and there
were at least a few who'd managed to elude
various stateside authorities and divorce lawyers.
And like her, they didn't really fit in well among
the kind of people who wore shoes and socks
all day.

So here she was, finally, where she really
belonged. Andrés, the *velador* who took care of
the house across the street, was a nice and
simple guy she could rely on to watch her house
too, if she needed to leave town for a few days. It
was a fine way to live out her waning years. She
had never much thought about it that way until
just recently and the realization that she was no
longer young and wild troubled her. "But watcha
gonna do?" she said, with a laugh.

An early boyfriend had referred to her as
"Anna Karenina." He was the kind of guy who
read ancient classics and he said that was his
fond nickname for her because it included her
name. But Karen wondered if there was a deeper
meaning and bought the Cliff Notes version so
she could try to catch up. After she got about
halfway through the short version of the novel
and knew a lot more about the complex life of
Tolstoy's famous character, she still didn't see
where it related to her. She felt it was some
snarky pseudo-intellectual comment, just a
cheap play on her name, and by this time she

wasn't sure she liked that boyfriend much anymore anyway, so she moved on with her life. And she still hasn't figured out what the convoluted life of Russian nobility had to do with her.

She had always been impatient and not much of a reader in school but she had a kind of street smarts that she was proud of and she didn't let anyone make her look foolish. She was once a sexy young thing, a challenge for the boys, and those smug college-bound boys were a particular annoyance, with their behind-the-back quips that seemed to make fun of her unschooled nature. They were especially ready to get into her pants and then disappear the next morning before their friends, and their regular girlfriends, saw them with her.

And now, in the age of instant internet fame, some girl named Karen had done something really stupid in public and any time another airhead fumbled her way onto the national stage she was also labeled a Karen. "Just my luck. Again," said Karen, with a sardonic laugh. "And watcha gonna do?"

It was about thirty years ago when Karen hitchhiked her way south into the Mexican desert along with another young female friend and a lady in her 50s who said it would be fun. There was no real plan beyond that. They got a few rides from bewildered Mexican workers who were not used to gringas thumbing rides by the road. But those guys were not going far from their local villages and their old vehicles did not appear up to a longer trip anyway. Finally a guy named Ray, from Iowa, picked them up in a big sedan and drove them to a little beach town he knew of, a town called Bahía Tiburón. Before something bad happened to them, he said.

Ray found a good restaurant when they arrived, and he shared a round of margaritas with them, plus a couple of platters of delicious fish tacos. And then he bid them farewell. Karen was not sure if she was relieved or disappointed when Ray said goodby without even trying to hit on any of them. It wasn't really the best thing for their self esteem, but they were probably a little road rough by that time and maybe not as appealing as they hoped.

So Karen and her friends pitched their bedrolls on the beach for the next few nights and got to know a little of the town. Using just a bit of the Spanish she recalled from a high school class, she jokingly referred to their bed-down as The Hotel Camarena, which translated to The Sand Bed Hotel. And she realized there was something about the place, about that simple roadside restaurant that had good tacos, the long, clean, uncrowded and sweeping beach, the view across the Sea of Cortez to a mountain on the distant Baja Peninsula. Now that really appealed to her.

After their big adventure south of the border, Karen returned to a working life in the States with fond memories of that little Mexican beach town. It was a beacon of hope, and she finally returned when she got close to retirement. She didn't have much money and no retirement income yet, but she knew she could figure out something. She always had in the past. As a guy she knew long ago had once said when he walked out of a job he hated, "I was looking for a job when I found this one!"

The town was different after so many years, but it hadn't changed enough that it mattered. And Karen hoped she could afford to live there for a few years until her Social Security finally arrived. It wouldn't be much, but she had always been resourceful and could probably figure a way to make it work, even without a partner to help with the bills. That had never worked so well in the past and she knew it probably wouldn't work well in the future. She had strapped on her tool belt at times in the past to eke out a few pesos doing odd jobs, and she could do it again. It would be just her and a shaggy mutt named Cazzie.

That scruffy little puppy had wiggled her way into Karen's heart long ago and they had traveled much of the western US together. Through several boyfriends, a couple of short marriages, and now this move to Mexico.

When Cazzie died Karen suddenly found herself without the best friend she'd ever had.

On late afternoons they had often climbed that hill with the shrine to the Virgen de Guadalupe for some quiet away time together, and just to look out over the Sea. Cazzie had always been there to lick her tear-stained cheeks after every personal setback, and now even she was gone.

The cardboard box containing Cazzie's body was heavier than Karen expected and she struggled with it up the hill where she had dug the grave. She covered the box with gravely dirt and piled large rocks on it to keep wild animals from bothering Cazzie's corpse, and then she sat down to wipe another tear from her cheek and look out into the sunset over the Sea of Cortez, just as she had many times before on this same hill with Cazzie at her side. Her friend was still there now beside her, but Karen's life had changed.

A mangy yellow beach dog saw her sitting on the hill and gave her tail a little hopeful wag, but Karen was having none of it. She wasn't ready to adopt another cute dog and then have it die, too, and break her heart again. It was too soon for any of that, if she even ever wanted to go through that again. Besides, the local dogs were covered in fleas and ticks and it would cost a few more pesos than she had to get all that taken care of. It was not an option on her tight budget.

She would return to the hill often, their special hill, just to pay homage to her close friend. And that scrawny sandy-haired beach dog was usually somewhere nearby. Then one day, the dog picked up a blue plastic flower that had been left by someone at the shrine, brought it over, and gently dropped it at her feet. Karen burst out crying. The dog, who would soon be named Lupita to honor the shrine where they met, sat there quietly with her as she cried. The sun slowly blazed a ruby pathway across the water and disappeared behind the distant island. Then Karen and Lupita went home together.

***

5

sidro showed up often *buscando la chamba,* looking for work involving his particular specialty, climbing Robert's tall ladder and trimming the palm trees. This time he was wearing a different T-shirt that he had just gotten at a *segunda,* one of the local secondhand shops that buy bags of clothing by the pound in the US for resale south of the border, and Robert laughed when he read the message on the front. He felt that it fit Isidro quite well, as he was known for enjoying life to the fullest, which often involved lounging under a shady tree and sharing a few tokes and some beer with the scruffy crowd he hung out with.

Robert had no problem with that because marijuana never killed anybody and it was far less harmful than the liquor he saw plenty of retired gringos putting away. And he always felt the whole Drug War was a phony deal anyway. It was nothing more than a wealth transfer system to make gun dealers and private prisons rich. Low-level pot users got busted, and the flow of actual hard drugs continued with nary a pause because there never was any real incentive to stop it. In fact, there was every economic reason to continue the game. And the Mexican government went along with the whole *Kabuki* theater act imposed by the DEA because they were never going to kill off one of the four or five main pillars of their economy. They just had to round up one of the more flamboyant kingpins now and then to put on a show that made some headlines and kept the U.S. taxpayers amused.

So the only thing the Drug Warriors have ever succeeded in doing is ruining the lives of many young people who got busted for smoking a joint and had that stain their records forever. Meanwhile, the rich kids and political hypocrites popped pain pills and snorted cocaine at their private parties. And the lucrative private prison industry stuffed their cells with harmless dope smoking minority kids who caused little trouble and were more profitable than hardcore criminals.

"It's disgusting. Those are nothing more than political crimes, and the victims are political prisoners," he said out loud now and then, to nobody in particular. Robert realized he could rail about this for hours even though nobody was listening. But it still annoyed the hell out of him.

None of this seemed to affect Isidro because there was no reason for the local cops to take an interest in his harmless activities. But Robert became more concerned about Isidro's habits when he showed up one day with a stainless rod screwed into the side of his left leg to hold the pieces of his broken bones together after he fell out of a tree he was working on. It took many months for him to recover, and Robert was relieved when Isidro declared that he was never again going to climb the tallest palms while he was stoned!

But Isidro was intrigued by Robert's reaction to his new T-shirt and asked, *"¿Que dice? ¿Que dice?"* What does it say?

Robert laughed as he translated the message into Spanish: *"Mota es la respuesta, pero no recuerdo la pregunta."* Or as it said in English, "Dope is the answer, but I don't remember the question."

Robert had been watching the gulls and pelicans diving into the Sea when an osprey snatched a fish from the water and flew right over the veranda to perch on that huge cardón cactus across the road where he liked to consume his catch. The bright yellow orioles were chirping in the nests they had woven carefully into the palm fronds high overhead. And one of the local Gila Woodpeckers landed on the side of a palm tree to squeak at him. It was his way of saying that the stone water bowl that Liz had repurposed as a feeder was empty and that Robert needed to pour out some more of that dog food he bought at the local store. The birds seemed to really like it, so there was no point in getting special bird food for them.

A house on the beach was definitely Plan A, the way Robert saw it. Anything else was Plan B, even though a few friends said they actually preferred to live a block or two off the beach where they saw plenty of lizards, rabbits, quail, bushy-tailed squirrels, javelinas, and coyotes. Jimmie Wilson had an interesting situation after he installed an alarm system around his property and something kept setting it off. He figured out the fig tree he planted was loaded with ripe fruit and the local coatimundis, a type of tropical raccoons, were hopping the fence to raid the tree. But things settled down after all the fruit was gone.

There were also more snakes back there, and that made Robert recall another encounter with a friend of his. But right then the woodpecker squeaked at him again as a reminder to refill the food bowl, and Robert said, "Yeah, ok, ok," as he rose from his comfortable seaside chair and headed inside for a scoop of dog food to make the birds happy again.

**

John, the Rattlesnake Rescuer

John had never actually considered becoming a rattlesnake rescuer before, but it just seemed to happen. He was a retired drummer who had played a lot of gigs in Las Vegas and did a mean version of "Wipeout," and now he was taking care of a local house for some friends who returned to the States every year during the hot Sonoran summers.

The summers can be brutal along the Sea of Cortez, with daytime temperatures remaining above 100°F for a couple of months, and with enough humidity lifted from the Sea to send rivulets of water running down the screen doors. The few gringos still around—the summer survivors who stayed in town—spent most of their time inside with the A/C on. Meanwhile, hardy Mexican workers struggled outside in the

heat, building beach homes for those with more
money than their workers would ever see. John
was amazed at their stamina and he felt guilty
just watching them at the various construction
projects when he took his usual morning walk
around town before the worst of the heat
descended on the land.

On his usual morning stop by the house of his
friends, John noticed a small rattlesnake curled
up in a cool spot in the back end of the pump
house to escape the heat, and then he stopped
by to see Robert and discuss the situation. The
snake was not being aggressive or threatening in
any way, but just hanging out where it was cool,
like any reasonably intelligent reptile in the
Sonoran summer heat. But John wasn't particularly
put at ease by Robert's attempts to reassure him
about the snake's benign intensions.

Robert knew that most snakes just find a quiet
place to rest up for a few days after devouring a
mouse or some other rodent, and he suggested
they just ignore the snake for a while until it
could wander off. But after a couple more days
the rattlesnake was still there by the cool water
pump, and they decided to deal with it before
the owners returned. Besides, John was
concerned that the snake might just hang around
outside somewhere after its long nap, and he did
not want to risk encountering it on a return visit.

Meanwhile, Robert had been thinking about
the problem and trying to come up with a

humanitarian solution. It was like Robert to
come up with some idea that was contrary to
what most folks would think of—which is just to
kill the damn snake and toss the body somewhere
out in the desert for the scavengers to deal with,
but only after showing it off to their friends so
they'd know how brave it was to kill a small
animal. Or something like that. But Robert
tended to think that snakes were here a long time
before he arrived and that he was the interloper,
not them. Hell, they were probably around here,
he figured, before the first humanoids ever
crossed over that land bridge from Asia around
10,000 or maybe 50,000 years ago.

Robert recalled another hot summer day
when he was on a little beach at a lake back in
New Mexico and walking slowly along the shore
through a tangle of driftwood. He was being very
careful where he put his bare feet to avoid
stepping on a sharp branch or a rock, when he
noticed one of the branches pull back from
where his foot was about to land. He was
leaning slightly forward when he realized it was
a rattlesnake that had been sunning itself on the
shore, and he quickly did a comical back-paddle
in the air with both arms to regain his balance.
After steadying himself and stepping back a few
feet he took several deep breaths and tried to
relax, but his heart was beating heavily. The
rattlesnake was still lying there quietly, trying to
blend into the branches, and had not recoiled to

strike, or even rattled its tail. Robert recalled that a snake can only strike the length of its body and he figured the snake was less than six feet long, so he sat down on the sand about six feet away from the snake to close his eyes for a moment, take a few more deep breaths, and regain his composure. And to talk to the snake.

"Well. You had me going there, fellow. And I sincerely want to thank you for being coolheaded enough to give me a pass this time. You had a right to defend yourself if I'd stepped on you, but you were quick enough to keep that from happening. And I thank you again for that.

"Each of us has his own special place in the grand order of things, in the greater environment," he continued as he waited for his heart beat to return to normal, "here on this modest shore of a minor planet lost in a forgotten corner of the cosmos. And you're fully entitled to your own special role on a piece of the grand domain, my scaly friend. This is your land, too, and there's plenty for both of us around here."

It was a one-sided conversation that Robert hoped would calm the snake as much as it calmed himself. And the snake listened quietly as Robert bumbled his way along onto philosophical territory. Robert had been a Philosophy major briefly in college long ago, before switching to the other lucrative career path of English major. He was glad now that his brief encounter with some of the great philosophers had prepared him for this moment, and glad also that he finally had a captive audience to share his musings. It was not lost on Robert that the snake seemed to be tolerating this long discourse better than any of his philosophy professors ever had.

After several minutes Robert felt at ease, so he rose slowly to his feet to avoid alarming the snake, and bid him farewell before wandering back down the beach in the direction he came from. It was a lesson in patience, of sharing a chance encounter with another of the beautiful and wonderful creations of strange providence, and of not jumping to easy conclusions based on the fantasies and phobias of his fellow humans.

But was all this concern really just based on unfounded phobias, phantoms, and boogymen, or were venomous snake bites a serious concern? Robert did the research later and found that very few people, only about five per year, actually die from poisonous snake bites, and most of those were messing around with their own poisonous pet snakes, or were involved in religious snake-handling rituals and then refused medical attention for religious reasons. So snakebite deaths are extremely rare.

A far larger problem is the 30 to 50 people who are killed each year by their own pet dogs, and an astounding number of them are children. And of course, the number of people—tens of thousands, actually—killed every year in car wrecks puts all of that in the shade. And then there are the mass shootings by morons with machine guns that were legitimized by a blatantly biased Supreme Court that willfully ignored the 2nd Amendment's requirement for membership in a "well-regulated militia." But that was a whole other subject that Robert, a former Marine, fumed about now and then.

So after all those musings, and his fond memories of a quiet rattlesnake encounter in another desert long ago, Robert came up with an idea—and he hoped it was a good idea—for dealing with John's snake problem.

When John came by again, Robert had a large plastic garbage barrel and a tight-fitting lid ready to toss into the back of John's truck. And he had a hoe to scoop the snake into the barrel.

But he also remembered a time when he was scrambling over some large boulders on a hot day to get to an overlook at the lava-crusted top of a plateau. He was the second person in the line of climbers and he suddenly heard the distinct loud warning of a rattlesnake that had been awakened by the first guy who crawled over a particular boulder. Again he was a bit off balance and cartwheeled his arms to avoid falling while he looked around for the snake. Then he heard it rattling from deeper in the crevices and realized it had crawled further down into the cool rocks to escape the climbers.

It was doing the sensible thing, to avoid trouble on a hot summer's day.

After he recalled that incident, he realized how important it was for the snake to find a safe place—a *querencia,* they call it in bullfighting—where he could feel safe, if not actually hide. So he tossed several orange foam life jackets into the plastic barrel that the snake could hide under and not feel exposed. Then he also could not strike out at them from the bottom of the barrel.

The snake was still drowsy when they arrived at the pump house, and Robert was able to carefully scoop it into the barrel. After briefly rattling its tail, it slid under the protection of the life jackets and settled in while Robert closed the lid. John and Robert were both surprised that the whole snake capture thing did not result in chaos and went as smoothly as it did, instead of the snake making a mad dash for the only open door just as both of them did the same.

It was a long bumpy ride on a dirt track far out into the desert, and the snake sometimes complained as the barrel jostled and bounced around in the back of the truck. But it mostly stayed quiet as John and Robert looked for a good place to empty the barrel—a place that would be safe for the snake, and attractive enough to keep him out there far away from any humans.

The hearty plants that live in the rugged and rocky lands of Sonora produce a lot of seeds throughout the year, and that feeds a lot of rodents, making it a suitable habitat for hungry snakes. John and Robert finally came to a stop at a sandy area where there were plenty of rodent tracks on the ground, and they lifted the barrel out of the truck. They carried it to a place where the sand was thickly covered with recent tracks, and then they looked at each other.

"You ready to run for the truck?" John asked skeptically as Robert began to loosen the lid and the snake made some of his complaints known.

Robert raised his eyebrows and glanced at John, then he flipped the lid off to one side and dumped the barrel over so the life jackets and the snake all spilled out on to the ground. Then they each took a couple of quick steps in the opposite direction, back toward the truck, in case the snake raised any objections to this new situation.

The snake paused to look around as he caught the whiff of fresh rodents, and then he tested the ground with his tongue and calmly slithered off into the bushes without looking at either of the humans behind him. They both watched in awe as that beautiful creature departed slowly, pausing often and carefully sniffing for the freshest trail. Then he blended into the sandy desert landscape under the bushes and disappeared as John and Robert smiled at each other. And they laughed in relief because they had each expected the whole thing to turn into a disaster. But it had all gone better than either of them believed was possible.

John rolled the drum over on its top and hand-played maybe his best-ever version of "Wipeout" on the upturned bottom, while Robert whistled along and did his own crude version of something strange that he called a "snake dance." Probably, they hoped, nobody was anywhere nearby to watch them out there acting like a couple of heat-demented fools in the deserted wastes of Sonora. But at the moment, neither of them really cared.

***

6

The cool morning sunlight slowly melted into a hot afternoon, and Robert thought about some of the odd and eccentric things they'd heard had happened since they moved here to this remote beach town, and other things people talked about that had happened in the earlier years before he and Liz arrived. For instance, that story about the US lady whose husband died here in Tiburón.

As the story goes, she did not want to have to deal with the complications of Mexican paperwork, or the expense of shipping the body north, so she propped him up in the car and headed for the border. When she got to the US Customs gate, about five hours later, the US Border Patrol asked for their passports, and she handed hers out the window. Then she said to her husband, "Hey dear, wake up. They need your passport. Hey dear, wake up." And she nudged him in the ribs. When he remained inert and slumped over to the side window, she shook him by the shoulder and said, "Oh my god! He must have died! I thought he was sleeping! Oh no!"

By that time, of course, they were on US territory, and she had figured it would be easier to deal with the problem there. The Border Patrol called an ambulance, and they took the body to a funeral home where he was cremated; then she took the ashes back to Kansas for a family ceremony.

Robert kind of wondered if rigor mortis might have set in during the several hours it took her to get to the border, or maybe he started smelling bad and the Border Patrol might have gotten suspicious. But he had no idea about that kind of thing regarding dead bodies, and besides, that level of detail would have ruined a perfectly good story.

There were so many stories like that in this town, and some of them were probably even true. Liz had said he should write some of them down in a journal, and he thought he might just do that some day.

It had not all been easy. Getting here, that is, to just hang out on a Mexican beach. And when he really thought about it, the whole idea that he could just hang out here on his own veranda like some rich guy in paradise seemed so improbable. Sure, he'd had that dream ever since he was a kid, but there had been so many roadblocks, sidetracks, and at least a few self-imposed disasters, along the way that he still couldn't figure out how it happened. When he counted up the times he'd left various jobs and faced other setbacks in life... well, that should have been an indication.

There were two times that he recalled in his distant youth when he'd worked his ass off as a dishwasher, and both times they'd handed him a paycheck after his shift and told him not to show up for the second day of work. It's hard to imagine being a worse failure than being fired as a dishwasher. He just sat on the curb and laughed as he stared at the pathetic little check he'd been handed.

In his twenties he was a crew boss on a new subdivision being built at the edge of town. It was in the middle of a cold winter, and on Monday morning none of the rest of his crew showed up. So he thought, "Aw the hell with it," and went back home to a warm cup of coffee. When he and his crew showed up the next morning, the superintendent quickly came by with their checks and told them all to beat it. Then he told Robert, "I was going to fire the rest of them and keep you, until you took off too." So Robert told him he was actually sick of freezing in the cold, anyway, and was heading to Mexico for a few weeks to thaw out. Back in those boom times he had the attitude that construction work was easy to come by, and it usually was. He only had to toss his tool belt into the back of his truck and show up at one of the many job sites around town. The foreman would check the quality of his tools and tell him to show up in the morning.

One of Robert's high school buddies went out looking for a job, and when the foreman asked to see his tools he said, "I've got a hammer and a tape, but I lost the tape." The foreman thought it was so funny he hired him as a laborer.

Robert's neighbor, Henry, was also from Albuquerque, and he was one of those right-wingers that Robert was sometimes surprised by. He was quite a bit older than Robert, and by this time he spent most of his days in front of the TV watching Fox Fake News And Other Assorted

Lies. But he had taken Robert fishing a couple of times, and they had a good time. They could get into politics without it turning nasty, but mostly they avoided the subject. Henry had come to Tiburón long before Robert and he'd never learned much Spanish, but he had a charitable heart and could even be generous when the need arose.

***

Henry

Henry walked over to the kitchen sink and looked out the window again. He couldn't remember how many times he'd looked out that window this morning, as if he actually expected something to happen in this small town, but he didn't really keep count. That would have been ridiculous. It's not like all that much ever happens anyway on the street in front of his house in this quiet Mexican village. Once in a while someone walked by, sometimes even a car went by. But it's the sort of thing he caught himself muttering as he looked out again toward the street, "I don't know how many times I've looked out this window this morning."

And that was another thing. He was muttering to himself often now since Doris died three years ago. He seemed to do that more lately, and he didn't like it. But the silence was deadly, as if madness were approaching if he didn't at least say something out loud now and then. It wasn't natural living with the silence, and there seemed to be something even threatening about it. He realized he'd never actually lived alone like this before. Probably not many people do before they're old and widowed, like he was now.

His coffee had gone cold again and now it tasted more like a mixture of mud and tar than coffee. Maybe his friend Marge was right; maybe there is a limit to how many times you can nuke a cup of coffee in the microwave before you ruin it completely. She tried to tell that to her husband John before he died last year, and she became one more of the "widder wimmen" here in Bahía Tiburón. Now he and Marge were often paired up at canasta parties and other events.

That's how life goes in your final years. You get paired up with some other old person and people say, "Oh, aren't they cute?" Some of his buddies had avoided that trap and had taken younger Mexican wives they could hardly talk to, but that didn't interest him. He poured his cold coffee down the drain and wandered back to the dining table.

The morning newspaper was still where he'd left it, so he sat down again to study some more. Trying to read part of the newspaper each day had been the only way he'd ever learned much Spanish. He started over again at paragraph seven of an article about a *feria de ahorros* put on by the *Comisión Federal de Electricidad*. It was a fairly boring article about how to save money on your electric bill, but he was making his way through it with a Spanish-English dictionary by his side.

The CFE was sponsoring events like this *feria* to encourage people to use efficient light bulbs, newer refrigerators, and the like. Mexico doesn't offer a volume discount for people who use lots of energy. Instead, they charge more per kilowatt-hour as the usage goes up, a sort of volume premium. They do it that way so poor people can afford to have a few light bulbs and basic appliances, and to discourage the rich from being wasteful. It made sense to Henry, and he noticed an immediate decrease in his bills when he replaced that old noisy refrigerator with a new one, and several old light bulbs with the new, more efficient LED models.

Henry heard the door open as Carmen came, in and she softly said, *"Buenos días."* She had missed the early bus again and was late. Again. And he wondered if that would ever change. Or if it was even as big a problem as it sometimes seemed. The whole *mañana* attitude was one of those things that attracted him to a Mexican retirement in the first place. He told friends that he'd fired her eight times, but she spoke no English, and he spoke too little Spanish to be understood. So here was Carmen again, arriving as usual, sometime on Tuesday, to clean the house. And maybe break a few more things in the process.

He realized that she'd actually taught him to relax whenever he heard the sound of another piece of memorabilia shattering against the floor. After closing his eyes, he'd take a deep breath and try to wipe it from his mind. His liberal daughter lived in the Bay Area and she called it the "zen of detachment," or something like that—a way of not valuing possessions too much. But that was easy for her to say, since she lived far away in the US and didn't have to deal with a clumsy old cleaning lady every week.

Henry went to the sink again to rinse his cup and put it on the drain board. He looked up through the window to see Maria, his very old Mexican neighbor, standing at the curb, leaning on her cane and looking down the street. This was her shopping day and she was waiting for the bus to take her into town. He'd known Maria since before she buried her first gringo husband. And then she married another one. After the second one passed away, she could choose between their two different US Social Security accounts for her own retirement. It allowed her to live a quiet, modest life in the village she called home. She had never learned to speak much English, but that didn't seem to be a problem with either of her husbands.

Henry stepped through the front door, picked up one of his old plastic chairs from the porch, and carried it to the street. "Here, Maria," he said. "Why don't you sit in this chair while you wait?"

Maria smiled, and said, "*Buenos dias, Enrique,*" and she pointed up the street as the bus came into view and slowed to pick her up. Henry liked it that she called him *Enrique.* As she boarded the bus she said, "*Gracias,*" and several other things in Spanish as the bus pulled away. Henry understood the words *mas tarde,* but not much else, as he put the chair back with the others on the porch.

He was almost resigned to never really learning to speak Spanish, especially the rapid way they slurred the words here in Sonora. And then there were all the local slang words that he could never find in any dictionary. Yet familiarity with a few Spanish words had seemed to make his life richer.

The crash of some small object hitting the floor jarred Henry from his thoughts. He resisted the temptation to turn around and see what it was, as Carmen quickly swept it up and took it outside to the trash. She seemed to know that Henry was unlikely to look in the dumpster on the corner and she could pretend it was not something important. She also wondered if Henry was losing his hearing, since he usually did not respond to the crashes of memorabilia anymore. Henry was hoping she thought that, although his hearing remained excellent for a man of his age.

They had become, Henry mused, just about like any other old couple who tolerated each other for lack of knowing what else to do. When Doris was still alive, there were some things they just stopped talking about, like his increasingly bitter political views. Doris was also frustrated by the daily corruption she witnessed in the news from back home but she didn't let it eat at her, like Henry did. In a way it was easier now with Carmen, since she had no idea what he was saying.

Carmen moved on to do the ironing, and Henry sat outside on his veranda facing the beach to watch swarms of birds dive-bombing on a school of small fish. The Sea of Cortez is a remarkable body of water, and one of the major migratory flyways of the world that provides an important source of food for millions of migrating birds. Each winter, shrieking hordes of birds descend on the small fish from the air, while schools of larger fish attack them from the bottom. Henry had spent years fishing this rich body of water long before GPS came along, and he still knew where all the X's were. He could stop his boat right over a sunken rock face 70 feet below and have a cooler full of fish in a couple of hours.

The boat was gone now. Doris was the one who knew the time had come to sell it when she saw how much difficulty he'd started to have with the hooks and reels and the boarding ladder and wondered what they'd do if something went wrong out there in bad weather. She had been with him through some heavy stuff when they were younger, some really bad water. And when she finally brought it up for discussion, he knew it was time.

But the shimmering waters still called to him, even at this age. The familiar sound of waves whispering over the shore remained a comfort. The rustle of a soft breeze in the palm trees reminded him why he'd come here long ago on vacation, and why he returned each year until he and Doris retired on this quiet coastline for good. The warm sunshine felt good on his old legs and the sounds of small waves brushing the sand were soothing.

He wondered idly what his hippy neighbor Robert was up to on such a nice day. Maybe he'd walk over there after Carmen left. A visit with Robert and Liz was always amusing. And different. They had probably come up with a new way to compost their vegetable waste or some other strange thing that Henry was not interested in. And that's another thing he actually liked about this small town, that there were plenty of eccentric people he never would have run into if he'd retired in the States.

Henry heard Carmen say, *"Lista,"* and he realized he'd fallen asleep for a couple of hours in the shade of his seaside porch under the warm Sonoran sun. She was finished now and waiting to be paid. He always wondered what he might find after she left, when he tried to locate a spatula or something else to cook dinner with. He never knew where things would end up, or why. Carmen would throw his clothes into the washer and then iron them without checking the pockets, so there were many Mexican bills that had been nicely laundered. And then ironed. But none were ever missing. Henry went to his desk drawer and drew out three one-hundred-peso bills that had been recently laundered and pressed.

Carmen said *"Gracias,"* in her quiet way. Henry knew her life was hard, with a husband who also worked hard when there was work but drank too much in his off-hours, and a couple of jobless boys who had moved back into the house with wives who refused to help her with the housework. She was a poor suffering Mexican woman, an old stereotype that still seemed to linger.

Carmen quietly closed the door as she left to catch the next bus, and a welcome silence descended on the house. Henry watched while she hobbled to the street and the bus pulled up to the curb. Carmen waited on the curb as old Maria made her way painfully down the stairs, returning from her shopping trip. Then Carmen slowly boarded the bus for home while Henry returned to his easy chair.

Soon, Henry heard the tapping of Maria's cane as she knocked at his door. He opened the door and tried to understand what she had to say. He finally realized she was saying she was ready now to take those chairs he had offered to give her earlier. They would look nice on her patio.

Henry said, "Uh…." and tried to explain again what he'd said earlier, that he'd only meant to lend her a chair to sit in to wait for the bus. But he didn't know how to explain all that in Spanish, and he soon thought better of it anyway. He smiled and said, "*Bueno,*" and realized again how nice it would be if he understood Spanish a little better.

He carried two of the chairs and followed Maria as she hobbled slowly across the street, and then he returned to get the other two. And he agreed they looked very nice on her patio. Then he went back to his home across the quiet street. He would be going to town in about a week and he would buy four more plastic chairs for himself.

***

Jonathan

Robert was driving east away from the Mexican coast with the rugged outline of a sun-blistered island rising above the sand dunes and ocean waves in his rear view mirror. He was on his way to the closest ATM, which happened to be inland in Los Campos, about 50 kilometers away. It was also the best way to get a decent rate on money exchange, so about every two weeks he would drive thirty miles to get money. And so did most

of the other gringos who live along this section
of the coast.

It was a bright sunny Sonoran morning in
January and the sleepy fishing village of Bahía
Tiburón was awake and busy with the day's
chores. As Robert pulled away from the only stop
sign on the main road through town, he saw a
slender Mexican man under a battered straw hat
standing beside the crumbling pavement with his
thumb out, waiting for the Costa bus, or better
yet, a friendly ride. His clothes were old and worn
and not too clean, as is usual among working
men here. Robert slowed and stopped just past
him, and he ran to the van. Robert doesn't mind
the thirty-mile drive and he doesn't mind driving
alone and trying to understand the rapid Spanish
on the radio station from the University located
an hour away in Hermosillo. But usually the
morning programs discuss education, or health
issues, or other topics he can't follow well. So he
often picked up hitchhikers on the way to
Campos. They needed a ride and he needed to
practice his Spanish at a basic level.

Robert leaned over to open the door and the
hitchhiker jumped into the passenger seat.

"¿A donde va?"

Robert asked the question in Spanish so he'd
show some familiarity with the language and set
his passenger at ease, although the question itself
was superfluous. Unless this guy worked at one of
the farms or ranches down some side road, there

really isn't much of anyplace else to go on this stretch of highway except to Campos.

"Campos," His new rider replied with a friendly smile, and stared out at the road ahead.

After he settled in, Robert pressed on the gas pedal and asked another question to keep the conversation going.

"¿Vive usted en Tiburón Viejo?"

He probably lived in the old Mexican settlement and not along the beachfront where the rich gringos live. He looked at Robert quizzically and asked, "Do you speak English?" He had a raspy, cigarette-and-whisky kind of voice. There was no trace of an accent, and it was clear to him that Spanish was a second language in this van.

The surprise must have registered on Robert's face. He glanced over at his passenger and briefly studied his dark weatherbeaten face, his stubbly chin, his dirty hat before turning back to watch the road.

"Yeah. Some," Robert said, stating the obvious.

"Well I couldn't tell if maybe you were French Canadian or somethin'." he replied.

He resembled another guy that Robert had picked up a few weeks back—a scrawny Mexican farmworker who was dressed about the same. The farmworker was looking for a job in the fields of Sonora because they paid 100 pesos (about $9.00) a day, and they only paid 70 in his home state of Sinaloa. He had walked from Los Campos

out to the coast to see about finding work with
the fishermen and he'd found nothing. When
Robert picked him up he was walking back
toward Campos to ask around the large farms in
the area.

He was surprised and happy that a gringo
would give him a ride and be interested in his
story. As they rode along he pulled out a picture
of his wife, his six beautiful young daughters, and
his mother-in-law back in Culiacán. After six girls,
they had finally given up trying to have a son. He
loved his family and wanted to be back in Sinaloa,
but had to leave to find decent work so he could
feed them all. He was grateful for the ride in a
clean passenger car and not in the back of a dirty
farm truck. He asked for nothing, but when they
got to Los Campos Robert handed him 50 pesos
to get some food.

At first glance this new hitchhiker had looked
almost like the same guy. He was dressed in an
old plaid cloth jacket, worn dirty jeans, and a
dirty hat. He was wrapped tightly against a cool
northerly breeze, although the temperature was
moderately warm by gringo standards.

But this hitchhiker was different. His name
was Jonathan and he lived in a rented shack
somewhere in Old Tiburón. He didn't offer to say
where and Robert didn't ask, although as they
spoke he was very forthcoming on most other
aspects of his life. Surprisingly forthcoming, in some

aspects. And when he said anything in Spanish, there was no gringo accent. Robert was puzzled.

"What brings you down here?"

"Well actually," Jonathan paused and laughed tentatively, "I'm on the lam for a DUI in San Diego. They were gonna give me two years, so I split for this side of the border. I always liked the people here in the village. I didn't think I could handle being in jail for two years."

Surprise registered again on Robert's face. He'd heard his share of bullshit artists in the past, yet detected none of that in this guy's story. He sounded like he was on the level, such as it was, and Robert was surprised at his openness about things most of us would rather keep to ourselves.

As they spoke, a bit more of his story unfolded. He had lived his first ten years with his father in the dirty mining town of Cananea in northern Sonora, and then in an Hispanic neighborhood of San Diego. He was completely fluent in Spanish. He'd been back to Mexico many times over the years, and now he was living a minimal existence on a meager allowance from his late parents' estate. He had no money for a car, and barely enough for food and shelter, but he was getting by alright.

Robert's partner Liz had once been hit by a drunk driver, so that DUI stuff didn't sit well with him. He nodded and stared at the road ahead. It was Robert's call. Would he stop the car and throw this guy out, or not? His passenger patiently watched the road, waiting for an answer to the question not yet asked. After a pause, Robert said that since he didn't have any money for a car, at least he wasn't driving down here, and maybe this was a good place for him to do penance instead of wasting the taxpayers' money back in California. He wasn't a big enough criminal for the US authorities to waste time on him so they'd probably just leave him alone, unless they caught him on that side of the border for some reason or other. And the Mexican cops probably didn't care that he was in their country without any legal paperwork. Robert had met other guys like him who lived in Mexico with no paperwork, and nobody seemed to care much about it. As long as they didn't cause any problems.

The stupid ones—the ones who still thought they were tougher and smarter than everybody else, despite all the evidence to the contrary— were the ones who usually got shipped back over the border. For a fugitive, Mexico offered a form of redemption, the chance to start a new life, if he was smart enough to see it. That nasty Ernie guy was a good example of stupid. He was hauled out of Tiberón by the Mexican cops after he went to extra lengths to make life miserable for a lady who tried to help him. The local newspaper said he was arrested "after attempting to cross the border." Yeah, after two big Mexican cops handed him directly over the border to two big US cops. The local newspaper saw no reason to brand little Tiberón with the scummy likes of Ernie.

Jonathan stared at Robert and listened, and said nothing. They rode in silence for a while. Robert got the sense that counselors far more proficient than he had failed to reach Jonathan in the past. Robert didn't think he needed to save people when they seem to be making it by themselves, so he also stopped talking and just stared at the road ahead.

Mexico is dotted with unfinished roadside projects and failed enterprises. This part of Sonora is no exception. They show up here and there on the road to Campos. Due to his long association with the area, Robert thought Jonathan might be a reasonable source of answers about a few of them.

"I've been wondering," he said. "What's the story with this old empty building on the left. Do you have any idea?"

"Actually no. I really have no idea. It's been there a long time, though. Looks like it's probably been empty for the last five years or so. I sure wish I could tell you, but I just don't know anything about it."

It seemed to be the first time Jonathan had ever noticed that vacant dilapidated building standing stark against the empty desert. It almost screamed to be seen, for the efforts of the builder to be not so easily forgotten. Robert remembered it clearly from his first visit here ten years ago, and it looked old then. He tried again a few miles down the road.

"This place on the right looks like someone had some grand plans, don't you think?"

"You know it sure does. I don't know what they had in mind there. Maybe a restaurant or something. It's really too bad. It looks like it could have been nice if they had finished it. Or maybe they finished it and it went out if business. But I just don't know."

Still no luck. Robert tried again a few miles later with a different subject.

"Those plants growing beside the road, with those big leaves, look a lot like castor bean plants. I suppose they could be left from a time when castor oil was still in demand and a lot of these abandoned-looking fields were probably planted with them. What do you think?"

"Well you know that probably does make sense. I bet that's probably true. I just don't know what those plants are. Could be castor bean plants, I guess. I don't know too much about plants. Actually I never noticed them before."

Every couple of miles for the rest of the trip Robert would ask a question or venture an opinion just to hear Jonathan say, "You know, that's probably true. I just don't know what the situation is with that," and so on.... Robert was fascinated by his apparent disconnection and complete lack of interest in his surroundings. Over the years he had managed to perfect a long and circuitous way of saying, "You know, I actually don't know anything about that, and I really don't even care." Robert had rarely encountered an individual who seemed so totally devoid of innate curiosity, who lived so completely in the moment—in whatever moment happened to exist in his head just then.

Jonathan was on his way to the bank in Los Campos to see if any money had been deposited in his account by anybody in his family. He needed to make a withdrawal at the ATM to pay some bills. The lady at the local *farmacia* in Tiburón could provide him with small amounts of money on his account, but she didn't keep much cash around. None of the local merchants did. It was also far less expensive to withdraw cash at the bank ATM than to borrow money from the merchants.

The dusty main street of Campos was abuzz with activity, as it always is. Heavy trucks carried produce from the fields, peddlers wheeled taco carts along the shoulder of the road, groups of school children wearing their clean school uniforms and multicolored backpacks walked to or from their half-day sessions. Robert and Jonathan stood in the ATM line with workers, peddlers, and small merchants drawing out just a few pesos for the day. The contrast between rich gringos and poor Mexicanos is nowhere more apparent than in a line at the only ATM in a small Mexican town with a few expats.

On the first of each month there's always a long line of Mexican retirees drawing their

monthly allowance, their *Seguro Social*. A good
photographer or novelist could read the history of
Mexico in the creased faces and gnarled hands
of the people waiting for their payments in long
ATM lines in every city and town throughout the
country. Robert once made the mistake of being
in line on the first of the month and had to wait
about an hour to get to the machine. The old
campesino just ahead of him was a handsome
man, wearing a clean, if frayed, shirt and simple
straw hat. They struck up a conversation. He said
that he gets 1500 pesos a month for retirement.
Most Americans have a hard time living on a
social security payment of 1500 dollars a month,
about ten times what this man had to look
forward to.

On the way back to the coast Robert heard
more of Jonathan's story. His dad was a successful
engineer who installed ore crusher equipment at
the mines in Cananea. He had four brothers who
were all successful businessmen. One of them has
a vacation home on the beach in Tiburón,
although he doesn't appreciate Jonathan's
infrequent visits to the house.

Jonathan was clearly the black sheep of the
family. His brothers don't approve of his
friends; but to hear him tell it, that hasn't had
much of an effect on him. And Robert got the
feeling that the efforts of many other people
over the years had also had little impact on the
choices he'd made in his life. The money he

was expecting hadn't arrived in his account. Robert left him at the stop sign when they returned to Tiburón, and watched as he headed down one of the dusty side streets to wherever he was living at the time.

On another day and another trip into Campos, Jonathan is standing by the road again waiting for a ride. He doesn't seem to recognize Robert when he gets into the van, but he recognizes the voice and realizes who his ride is. He explains that he doesn't see well without his glasses, which he managed to lose recently.

"I can't find them anywhere. I was telling one of my buddies," he explained, "that I needed to get to Hermosillo and get a new pair of glasses. And he said, 'No you don't. They're at my house.' And then I remembered that's where I was when I passed out from drinking last week. The problem is, I don't know his name. And I don't know where he lives. And without my glasses, I can't find him. I walk up to guys who look about like him and I squint at them, and they think I'm weird until I explain the problem."

Robert begins to think that maybe his brothers have a good point about not liking his friends. Or probably most of the choices he's made in his life. Or even having him stop by for a visit now and then. Jonathon rides to Campos again to see if his money has arrived yet. It hasn't.

A week later, on a bright Sunday morning, Robert rides his bicycle over to Old Tiburón to watch a baseball game between the local Bravos and the Mayos from Los Campos. The Bravos used to be the Tiburones, the "sharks," but they got a good deal on some shirts that read "Bravos" so they changed their name. Robert hadn't seen any sharks lately in the waters around the town that was named for them, but some of the local expats still wear their Tiburones caps because they like being thought of as sharks, especially at the weekly poker game in "Harley" Jackson's garage.

When the Mayos don't show up for the game, the Bravos use the afternoon for batting practice, and Robert leaves to ride along a few dusty back streets, to pause at interesting little homes that he doesn't notice when he drives a car through the old village. Many of these people have done wonderful things with a little concrete and a paint brush. They deserve a lot of respect for their ability to make a decent life and keep their kids in clean clothes for school, while they live in cardboard shacks. And some shacks, crudely decorated with simple painted designs, show the undefeatable spirit of an artist within.

Robert makes the long ride back to his place on the beach. It's a sunny day and there's a slight headwind. The azure sea is topped with small waves that break gently on the shore.

After a few miles of hard peddling, he stops to study some of the houses that line the road. He rests in the shade of a well-proportioned entryway fashioned of *cantera* stone, trucked up from Jalisco in large pieces and carved by local backyard craftsmen using chisels and grinders. In the next block he passes a nicely planted courtyard with tall coconut palms, their long graceful fronds clattering in the light breeze—a coconut wind. A few blocks later there's a bold red wall that resonates in this land of strong primary colors.

A brightly painted mailbox reminds Robert of a friend who once stopped by their house to pick up a recipe and then drove off without knocking at the door. Liz waited for a few minutes before giving her a call to inquire why she didn't knock.

"Well, I saw Buzón written on the mailbox," she said, "and I thought it was the Buzón family casa."

After Liz explained that *"buzón"* means mailbox in Spanish, she returned for the recipe.

Once in a while he passes someone walking along in the parking lane or waiting for the Costa bus to come by. The parking lane is safer than the crumbling sidewalk where you could easily break a leg or run into a low tree limb or a pipe sticking out from a house. He passes a dark, wiry fellow who looks vaguely familiar, but continues on for half a block before he realizes it's Jonathan, who's standing by the road again waiting for somebody, or something, or maybe nothing, really. Driven by probably morbid curiosity, Robert can't help but wonder what he's waiting for. He pulls up and circles back.

Turns out Jonathan finally figured out where he was when he passed out last week and lost his glasses.

"I talked to the guy and he said he'd be here in half an hour, and that was an hour or two ago," he says with an exasperated laugh that has now become familiar. The nervous laugh of the perpetual victim—victim of his own devices and years of poor choices. Life's a bitch when you have no money, no prospects, little respect, and there's no good reason anyone's going out of their way for you anymore. At least anybody who knows you well.

So Robert shares a noncommittal laugh with Jonathan, wishes him luck, and makes his way onward down the road to home. Jonathan doesn't need help. He has more highly developed coping skills than most of us ever manage to acquire. He'll be fine. And deep down, Robert realizes he's actually envious of this guy's multi-cultural agility, his ability to transcend social and ethnic cultures, and somehow survive. Robert rides away, knowing he'll see Jonathan again someday, waiting for a ride somewhere along the road to Campos.

***

Hank and Thelma Visit Huatabampito

Hank unhitched the car he was towing and parked it at the side of the road, then he put the big RV into reverse and carefully backed all 40 feet of it into the slot they'd rented for the night. He'd gotten pretty good at maneuvering the huge, bus-like vehicle since they bought it last year, and this time he'd nailed it right down the center of the slot. He kind of felt he ought to get a gold star or something each time he did it so perfectly, but that was childish and he knew Thelma would be quick to point that out if he ever mentioned it. Still, it made him feel like, well, a trucker, or something. And that seemed important, for some reason.

With the rig parked, it was time to explore the area a bit. This was their first visit to Huatabampito. Last Fall there had been a guy in Bahía Tiburón who talked up the place and said there were beachfront lots available for only $13,000. It sounded like probably the last undiscovered stretch of Mexican beach along the whole West Coast. In fact, it sounded too good to be true. They decided to check it out.

Actually, it was Thelma who wanted to check it out. Hank was happy living on the beach in Bahía Tiburón. They had a nice modern home with a long veranda that overlooked the Sea of Cortez, and with nightly, picture-worthy, sunset views over the Big Island. When they had friends over, most would linger on the veranda and study the Sea, even though they also had homes on the beach. Hank had taken so many gorgeous sunset pictures in the past that he didn't even bother anymore.

On quiet evenings, he liked to look out at the distant islands where he'd spent his younger years fishing before he sold the boat. And he liked knowing that the old volcanic cone you could barely see over on the Baja just above Santa Rosalia was 107 miles away, according to the GPS he had just bought. Hank wasn't sure he wanted to find a bargain beachfront lot farther down the coast. Since they'd arrived in Huatabampito, he'd only seen one semi-substantial building—a seafood restaurant. And it didn't look all that old, or all that well built. What villages he'd seen along the way were simple, agricultural, flimsy— and they were well inland. The beach area looked mostly deserted, like a barren coast, unprotected by the Baja, exposed to the full force of the ocean. One that probably got wracked by hurricanes, now and then. Maybe that's why nobody lived along the coast around here.

Hank walked around the RV to make sure it looked ready for the night. There were only two other RVs in the place and the whole area was quieter than they'd expected, except for the sound of the ocean. They locked the RV and got into the car to drive south down the long sand road that led

onward from the RV park, with the wide Pacific
Ocean thundering onto the broad beach that lay
off to their right. The ocean was louder here than in
Tiburón, Hank thought to himself.

The afternoon sun sparkled across the water
like a million liquid diamonds, and the November
onshore breeze felt refreshing and cool after a
long summer. Thelma stared at the diamond-
crusted surface of the water while Hank drove,
and wished again that she could capture it in
paint. She'd tried many times but it just wasn't
that easy. It was one of those things that separated
the Masters from the beginners. She wondered if
she'd ever get water right.

They passed a stand of coconut palms with
long fronds that swayed gracefully in the wind,
as coconut palms do. There were no other trees
as far as they could see, nothing but a long
sandy road stretching toward the horizon. They
knew there was an estuary up ahead someplace
at the end of the road, but they didn't know how
far it was. Thelma had brought her sketch book,
in case they found it. As in most places in
Mexico, there was little signage. The local
people didn't need signage to find the estuary,
and they didn't think there was enough tourist
interest to justify the effort. And even in places
that were overrun with tourists, there still
seemed to be little interest in signage. It was one
of the things that Hank especially liked about the
country. Traveling in Mexico meant you had to

be more self-sufficient and flexible than tourists who stayed north of the border.

Up ahead they noticed a vehicle on the road, coming fast in their direction. It was a white Jeep, that sped toward them and then quickly past. It looked new and expensive, with a fancy roll bar and Sonora plates. A youngish man was driving, with three girls aboard. They were laughing and seemed not to notice Hank and Thelma. Hank winced a little, to himself. He'd never had a fancy new Jeep when he was that young. Especially one with three girls aboard. He'd been a working stiff who'd done things, more or less, as society had expected. He'd spent some time as a rebellious young man, with a cool 1949 Ford two-door sedan he'd bought off a used car lot, but he'd never had enough money to be a playboy. Like that guy in the Jeep full of girls. He felt a twinge of jealousy.

The road led onward to the estuary somewhere up ahead, and they drove toward it. Or somewhere in that direction. Hank glanced over at the ocean, broad and blue, and remembered his Navy days. For an Arizona kid, the Navy was a life changing experience. He'd never seen so much water before he arrived at boot camp in San Diego. And when they shipped out to Hawaii on his first ship, and then on to the Far East, it was days and days of nothing but water. And now, every time he saw the ocean he still remembered the overwhelming vastness of it. It's impossible to understand the ocean, he thought, unless you've crossed it by boat or ship.

They drove onward, through scattered leaves. Or something.... Wait, thought Hank absently to himself, that's a twenty dollar bill lying there on the sand. And another one, and another one. The road was covered with them. Hank braked to a halt as he and Thelma looked at each other with their mouths hanging open. "What the...?"

As they got out, Hank started picking up bills by the handful. He and Thelma looked at each other again, each searching the other for answers. Thelma picked up a large blue zipper cloth binder containing a notebook that was lying open amongst the bills, and she thumbed through pages of carefully noted expense records. The cost for a hotel in Ciudad Obregón, a meal in Los Mochis, probably a couple of months of records, all in Spanish. There were lots of entries with names, but she had no idea what they meant. By now Hank had counted about $6,000 in twenties, which he arranged in piles on the back seat of the car, and he was still scooping up handfuls of them. After topping out at a bit over $10,000, Hank stood there and looked at Thelma.

"What do we do now?" he asked, as he glanced up the deserted road.

"Whose money do you think this is?" asked Thelma.

"How would you know?" asked Hank, "Who could have lost this much money?"

Hank realized he'd never had ten thousand dollars in his hands before. Actually right there in front of him. Right there, literally, in his hands. He realized he was breathing quickly, less from the effort of scooping them up than from the sheer terrifying thrill of discovery. It was a heady moment that Hank was completely unprepared for. And neither was Thelma. A hundred thoughts went through their heads. Probably a thousand. Was it drug money? I mean what else could it be? It could be somebody's vacation money. Or construction money, if they were gringos building a house in Mexico, like Hank and Thelma had done. But the notebook was all in Spanish. What are the chances the notebook had fallen out of someone's car entirely separate from these piles of twenties lying all around it? Should we just shut up and keep it? Shouldn't we turn the car around and get out of here? If it's drug money, it probably has cocaine all over it. If we keep it, we'll be busted at the border by drug-sniffing dogs, if we have any of it with us. Maybe they're all marked bills. And should we even consider keeping it? Are we that kind of people? It's a lot of money. If we keep it, will it put us into situations we can't begin to handle? Would the money be worth it? Are we into something that's way over our heads here?

Thelma stuffed all the bills neatly into the large notebook and zipped it shut. She put it on the back seat and threw a towel over it. They looked around. There was nothing but sand except for those palm trees in the distance. The road was deserted. Still, had someone seen them? Was there a reason why someone jettisoned the money?

They got in the car and drove on toward the estuary. They glanced at each other for answers, for a plan. Then they drove for a while in silence, each staring at the road ahead.

"We really don't need this money," Hank finally said. He was still staring at the road. "We don't know where it came from. We're doing fine without it. We don't need the trouble."

Thelma was relieved. That much loose money had scared her from the start. Had anyone seen them? They and that white Jeep were the only cars on the road. If it belonged to that guy, and he wanted it back, he'd have no trouble figuring out who found it.

Hank and Thelma had retired in Mexico, about half a day's drive north of Huatabampito. They had a reasonable pension and Social Security to live on. Their living costs, when they stayed in Mexico, were only about half of their income. That left enough extra to travel on, now and then. They really didn't need anything more. They had a good life. In fact, the whole experience of finding all that money had begun to turn a pleasant day's drive into a nightmare for Thelma. She suddenly felt the need to get rid of the money somehow. But how? If they gave it to the local

Policia, it would likely disappear into a pocket or two. But worse, they might end up in some kind of long-term legal hassle with the local cops. Every instance they'd heard of where a gringo had gotten involved with the *Policia* had turned out badly. Their Mexican friends and neighbors didn't trust the police either and avoided contact with them. It was a Pandora's Box they didn't want to open. They drove onward. Where was that damned estuary, anyway?

Hank slowed the car to a stop and stared straight out the windshield at the empty sand road ahead. "Do you want to see the estuary?" he asked.

Thelma took a breath and softly said "Not right now." Neither of them could focus on anything other than the $10,000 sitting on the back seat in the large zippered notebook under a towel.

Hank turned the car around. So far neither of them had a plan. Maybe they'd just keep the money until they could figure out what to do with it. There didn't seem to be any other possibility. Other than just pitching it out the window where they'd found it, and letting somebody else deal with it. Maybe one of the poor local fishermen would find it and start a new life. Or maybe it would ruin his life. Like those idiots who win millions in the lottery and end up bankrupt a few years later. Having all that money sitting on their back seat had suddenly seemed like a very bad idea.

They drove back in the direction they'd come. Neither of them knew what to say. Hank noticed a car far ahead, driving slowly down the road toward them. Soon he could see it was the white Jeep. The girls were walking beside the Jeep, searching for something, while the young man drove. He turned to stare at their car.

"Pull up next to them," said Thelma.

Hank stopped next to the Jeep. "What are you looking for?" he asked.

The driver answered in a torrent of excited Spanish, and Hank heard the word *azul*, and he thought he heard a word he recognized as meaning notebook, a word that Rosa, their housekeeper used to describe school supplies for her kids. The driver looked around at the empty sandy landscape. Then he stared hard at Hank, and added reluctantly and tensely, *"¡Y mucho dinero!"*

Thelma needed no more translation. "Is this it?" she asked, and held up the blue notebook. Hank and the young man both looked toward her, their mouths hanging open.

"¡Oh sí, sí!" the young man answered and quickly opened it, noting with relief that the money was still there. *"¡Muchas gracias!"* he said and paused for a moment in thought, eyeing the old retired gringos. Something about the way he looked at them made Thelma swallow hard. She wasn't sure why. She heard Hank take a deep breath. Then the young Mexican quickly pealed off five twenties and handed them to Hank.

126

"¡Muchas gracias!" he repeated, without smiling. The girls climbed back into the Jeep and they drove quickly away.

Hank and Thelma sat there staring down the road at the disappearing Jeep, a thousand thoughts racing through their heads. Thoughts about what could have been. What they could have done with all that money. Whether they should have kept the money, after all—yet recalling that steely look in the young man's eyes. But it was over now and the whole thing just needed a rest. There was too much left to think about. They needed time to digest it. It had all happened too quickly. Hank felt something like a chill deep in his spine, and he gritted his teeth for a moment. Slowly, they each breathed a sigh of resignation. Heavily mingled with relief.

Hank finally broke the silence.

"You want to go see the estuary?" he asked.

"No," said Thelma. "I think I need a drink."

***

Hank and Thelma were some of Robert and Liz's best friends in Tiburón and Robert loved retelling that story to friends over a round of cold margaritas. Robert and Liz had rented Hank and Thelma's home for a month at a time over several years before they retired and made the move to Tiburón. It had been available in the summer and fall because Hank and Thelma would take off for long road trips in their big class A motorhome during the hottest months. So Robert and Liz didn't even meet them for years, but they would leave notes of appreciation every time they headed back north to work in hopes they'd be first in line to rent it the next year.

It's the house where Robert wrote for hours and Liz spent lots of time sketching, where they took long lazy swims at dusk and wondered if one day they might even be able to retire and move there. And it's the house where they met up with their first hurricane. It's where they were staying when a friend knocked on the door one afternoon and said: "I hear you might be looking for a place on the beach...." And that's how they happened to get themselves a place on the beach not far from Hank and Thelma.

They shared home cooked suppers, made even better by Hank's dangerous margaritas, and stories were told as the sky transformed into those unbelievably stunning Tiburón sunsets.

But now Hank was gone. Lost too soon to the one of the many forms of cancer that are always ready to harvest the elderly. And now they were all getting older. That's one of the problems with living with a lot of retired folks. They're a dying breed, and they just keep leaving.

7

R obert and Liz had a card table, four feet square, with rusted metal legs, and four plastic chairs, that served as patio furniture on their shaded veranda overlooking the Sea of Cortez, although the setting probably deserved something better. It was a quiet weekday evening and the tourist families were gone until the coming weekend, so Robert brought out a tablecloth, two place settings, their last two unbroken stemless wine glasses, and the two battery-operated LED candles that usually sat on the table inside. Liz smiled when she saw how romantic, and also a bit ridiculous, it looked. These simple things were how they coped with the endless COVID lockdown, and they knew how lucky they were to be retired in a tiny Mexican beach town for the duration.

They relaxed after a fine dinner of pasta with chicken and roasted vegetables, and Robert poured them each a bit more wine from a bottle of good Mexican red from the Valle de Guadalupe, over on the Baja near Ensenada. After dinner they faced their chairs toward the water as the last dim light of the evening played upon the Sea and highlighted the distant mountains of the Baja Peninsula, and they shared a bar of dark Mexican chocolate while Robert remarked that the evening's dinner music—that gentle rolling of waves upon the shore—had surely been inspired by "La Mer," courtesy of Maurice Ravel.

The subject of how they'd managed to end up here— a common subject, an endless subject—came up again, and they discussed how important it was that they each had managed to grasp enough interesting opportunities along the way that somehow their paths had collided in the process.

"As they say," Robert tossed out in his usual snarky male way, "When opportunity knocks, you have to grab it by the balls and drag it in the door."

And Liz replied, "Yeah, that's how I scored you."

Robert glanced over to see her give a fist pump that said, "Yes!" better than words could ever say, and he knew she was still the girl who'd challenged and captivated him years ago. It still surprised him that she thought she was the lucky one to capture him, when he always felt that she was way above his social and intellectual level and he'd somehow tricked her into sharing his dubious schemes. And he knew again that none of the unfortunate victims of his past several prolonged affairs and failed marriages would have thrived on, or even survived, the numerous exciting and creative twists of his three-plus decade relationship with Liz.

When Robert was about six years old, his grandmother was serving ice cream and she asked him if he wanted "not enough" or "too much." Robert quickly said, "Too much!" And his grandmother retold that story often for the next thirty years until she passed away.

And now, as he and Liz sat with their wine on the veranda of their modest place on the beach, he realized that he really did have "too much" in his life.

Something about the quality of the early evening light caused Robert to realize what time of the year it was—almost Easter, and they could look forward to the beach soon being crowded with families happily spending their break from school and work, sharing the beauty that was part of Liz and Robert's daily life. Easter is an important religious holiday for the Mexican people, and it is celebrated in many ways.

Robert thought back on an Easter soon after they moved to Tiburón that gave him and Liz a treasured glimpse into the importance of religious rituals to their new neighbors.

***

Cenizas

Jack was knocking at the door. He and Peg lived two doors away. He had come to see if Robert and Liz could help deliver *cenizas* to a few of the more remote fincas and ejidos on the upcoming *Miércoles de Ceniza*, Ash Wednesday.

Both Robert and Liz had grown up in moderate Protestant families, but they each had long ago drifted from the fold. Now they pretty much

considered themselves atheistic, when they even
bothered to think about such things. They knew
nothing about quaint Catholic customs of smearing
ashes on foreheads at Easter-time, and various
other church rites.

So Robert told Jack, "Uh well, we're not
Catholic."

Jack said, "You got a car?"

And Robert replied, "Uh."

So Jack said, "You're Catholic enough. I need
you at the church on Wednesday morning at 9:00
a.m. We're going out, too, and Padre Pablo will give
us the ashes and our destinations. He'll send
somebody with you who knows what to do. See you
there on Wednesday." And he was out the door.

Jack was always refreshingly brief and to the
point. Robert had already guessed that Jack was
there to rope him into something, because that was
Jack's way. He was always looking to improve the
lives of people in the community, and he did a
very good job of involving any of the expats who
seemed to have extra time on their hands. Which
would be most of the expats.

After living in Tiburón for more than thirty years,
Jack and Peg still spoke almost no Spanish, but
they were longtime members of the local Catholic
Church and knew Catholic rituals well enough to
follow the priest at mass on Sundays. Their
youngest daughter attended local schools and was
fluent in Spanish, so she would be their interpreter

for delivering the cenizas. And since Padre Pablo was a sort of circuit priest administering to a large number of scattered communities and settlements, he needed some help to get the whole ashes thing done on Wednesday. Since Liz spoke decent Spanish, Jack knew she and Robert would do okay figuring things out for themselves. And that was actually okay with Robert because it sounded like another sort of adventure that would give them a deeper look into the daily life of back-country Sonora.

At 9:00 a.m. on the morning of Ash Wednesday, Robert and Liz were seated on the old wooden pews of the local church as sunlight filtered in to illuminate dust motes floating in the silent air. There was a short introduction and a prayer. Robert and Liz watched the others who were present and copied their responses. Then Padre Pablo gave everyone their instructions, in Spanish, and handed out maps to their destinations. The maps were really just rough hand-drawn sketches on notebook paper showing the more-or-less location that Robert had to find. They headed for their van as he tried to figure out which way on the map was north.

Liz saw that Robert was already enjoying himself with a new puzzle, so she focused her energies on comforting the two little middle-aged Mexican women who were sitting nervously in the back seat of the van. Their names were Maria and Rosa, and when they realized Liz spoke good Spanish, they opened up and long conversations began.

Maria and Rosa had known each other since childhood, had rarely left the village, and knew most everybody in town. Even the few they weren't related to. They felt it was a great honor to be entrusted with the ashes bestowed by the Padre, and Rosa clutched the little cardboard box safely on her lap like a chest of golden sovereigns.

Before long they were about 15 miles out of town and had made several turns that were indicated on the map when they passed a rough sort of gate at a dusty road that seemed to be the turnoff they were seeking. Robert backed up on the empty pavement and turned down the lane as heavy dust swirled up and created bold patterns on the side windows, and they all quickly raised their windows. It had been a dry year so far, but he had not seen anything quite as strangely spectacular as this. There seemed to be a foot-thick layer of loose dust between their wheels, and it created a choking cloud that billowed up around the van.

Soon enough they were at the *Ejido San José* where a smiling young girl about 10 years old flagged them down and asked who they were. The ladies in the back of the van explained they were bringing the ashes provided by the priest, and the young girl excitedly pointed toward a small adobe chapel that was about a block away. She ran ahead of the van and picked up a piece of rusty

steel to ring the community's bell—a large piece
of iron, possibly off an old truck, that was hanging
from a rough crossbeam. It gave out a string of
satisfying clangs that echoed over the desert. Then
she told them to wait at the chapel while she
spread the word.

The chapel was a simple shed of adobe walls
with a sagging and rusted metal roof and a dirt
floor. The walls were eroded in places where the
roof leaked, and at one end there was a simple
altar made of concrete blocks and a board.

Robert and Liz had never been to an *ejido*
before, and they studied their surroundings
surreptitiously while trying not to appear nosy. The
ejido system in Mexico was instituted after the
Revolution to continue a long-time custom of
community property usage that dated to before
Aztec times.

But in recent years there had been efforts to
dismantle various *ejidos* as developers and
politicians coveted those in prime locations,
especially in beachfront areas, where the land
could be sold to gringo expats. And there were
economists at the national level who made the
case that Mexico would be better off if they
concentrated on building a strong technological
base, and making the country's food production
more efficient to support the growing cities.

The *Ejido San José* was a sort of community
ranch located in a dry piece of desert that
appeared to be a stretch of leftover and forgotten

land that nobody else really wanted. The
settlement at the heart of it was a small collection
of modest adobe homes cobbled out of the dirt by
hard-working people who wanted a piece of
freedom and were willing to toil beneath the harsh
Sonoran sun to get it.

Soon the young girl, whose name was Sarahi,
returned in her cleanest once-white dress, followed
by other folk of various ages. Even as young as she
was, Sarahi seemed to be a natural leader, an
organizer who could take charge of an event.

As they all crowded into the tiny chapel, Maria
quietly asked Liz, "¿Y ya, que hacemos?" ("What
do we do now?")

Liz glanced at Robert and mumbled, "Uh well,
we don't know because we're not even Catholic."

The answer seemed to surprise Maria and Rosa,
that there might be people around who actually
weren't Catholic. They glanced at each other and
stood there, with Rosa clutching the box of
precious ashes.

Liz decided to ask young Sarahi if she was
familiar with the ceremony, and then Sarahi
proceeded to lead the group through the process
as best she could remember from last year's
service. At times another person in the small
group might remind her about a part she had left
out, and the ceremony would proceed onward.
Soon the faithful were getting their foreheads
properly smudged from the box that had been

given by the Padre, then filing back outside toward their simple homes.

A girl near the end of the line stepped forward with a small piece of torn paper to ask for a tiny amount of ashes. She wanted to take them to to her *abuela* who was bed-ridden in their little *casa*. Maria took a pinch of ashes from the box and set it in the center of the paper, and the young girl carefully folded the paper wrapper over it and headed home down the dusty road.

As Robert drove the van back to town, he and Liz noticed how good the main street looked after the annual effort to fix the *baches,* the potholes, and re-stripe the lanes before *Semana Santa.* It would look good for about the next three months before it all deteriorated again.

They discussed what a simple gift it had been for them to be part of Ash Wednesday at an old *ejido.* It had also been a meaningful event for the people they met—one that Robert and Liz helped make possible by sharing their time and their van for the occasion. And it was one more of the many lessons they learned each day by just living in the fascinating country of Mexico.

They dropped Rosa and Maria off back at the church in Old Tiburón and headed home. Robert was quiet for a while, then he turned to Liz and said, "You know, I'd really like to do this again next year."

***

8

Robert had been writing for years—bits and scraps that he wondered if any of it would ever amount to anything. But it was an obsession. Maybe he should use some of his time here on the beach putting something together, but he wasn't sure he even had the drive, or the talent, to finish anything that wouldn't read like a cheap novel. Or maybe he should just toss all that stuff in the trash and concentrate on doing next to nothing. Most of his retired buddies seemed happy doing nothing of importance, so why not give it a try? Maybe go play some pickle ball, that new game that's been going around, and share some stupid jokes. Guys had been doing that for a million years, playing goofy games with rocks and sticks or whatever was handy. And telling stupid jokes.

He dug out something he'd begun writing a few years back and read through it again, and then put it away. Again.

So why is this writing thing so damned difficult, he wondered. Sometimes he felt that English was only his second language, and that he never really had a first language. Damn.

Still, Robert liked to consider his own modest place within The Great Conversation, the ancient discussion described by Robert Maynard Hutchins that began long before Plato and his student Aristotle crafted the outlines of philosophy, and that continued onward through Copernicus, Kepler, and Einstein, to the deep thinkers of today, although he knew he was being a bit pompous to add himself to that group. But even the greatest Greek philosophers had built on the work of scientists and philosophers who posed those same great questions long ages before them. Each of them had built upon a foundation laid by predecessors they never met, and whose work was lost in the ravages and endless wars of time. We only know about them today through vague references jotted down by someone else much later in history. That wisdom was passed down mostly by word of mouth, and they all advanced the scope of human knowledge to the ridiculous point where Robert can laze around on his veranda in Mexico and look up arcane references to Arthur Rimbaud and other obscure symbolist French poets on his iPhone. It doesn't seem fair to make it that easy, but that's how it is these days.

Somehow this all made him think of his philosophical friend Nacho.

Nacho was the kind of guy that, well there was just something about him, something that Robert could relate to, something they had in common, a kind of shared heritage that involved a love of great literature and the lessons of history. Although they had grown up in different cultures, somehow it was the same culture—a culture of great literature and the arts. And they had a common language, even though Nacho spoke Spanish with a only smattering of English, and Robert spoke English with a dusting of Spanish. Conversations with Nacho reminded Robert of reading *All Quiet on the Western Front* in his teenage years. It was written by a German veteran of the brutal First World War, and Robert realized there were millions of young men killed on each side who had far more in common with the soldiers they were killing that they did with the generals and politicians who had led them into such a meaningless war. That book broadened Robert's global perspective, and he began to realize there were people in every culture who were his natural allies, his companions, regardless of the fact that many of them spoke languages unintelligible to him.

Later, as Robert contemplated his own possible fate in the meaningless Vietnam War, he read the poems of Wilfred Owen, a young British officer who had perished in the senseless First World War. And he wondered why nobody during all his years of education, from elementary school through high school, had ever mentioned Owen's insightful work. And especially his poem entitled "Dulce et Decorum Est," which exposed the grand patriotic lie of the Roman orator Seneca: "Sweet and Proper it is to Die for One's Country."

***

The Paleontologist

Nacho was not the first to notice the strange vehicle that entered the village that morning. He

was in his workshop carving a delicate design into
a headboard for a wealthy lady from the city and
he heard the car when it passed his open door but
he did not look up. It was Pablito, son of Pablo the
gardener, who had first seen the mud-encrusted
truck with the *placas* from *Meecheegan*. Pablito
was not sure where that was, but he had a feeling
it was far away from the village. He watched as it
turned down a dusty side street and stopped in
front of the old *casa* where Rosa Marquez lived.

A young, bearded gringo stepped from the car,
took a deep breath and stretched his back, then
stood for a moment before walking to the vine-
covered wooden gate into the courtyard. A heavy
branch from a large tree inside the courtyard
arched over the wall and provided welcome shade
as he stood for another moment studying the heavy
gate, almost as if he was afraid to touch it, to
disturb the silence of a tranquil dusty day. Then he
inhaled again deeply, reached up to grasp the bell
cord, and gave it two short tugs. The crisp sound of
the old brass bell broke the morning quiet and
seemed to announce his arrival to the entire
village. He swallowed nervously and glanced at
Pablito and a few of the other kids who were now
standing together under a tree on the other side of
the road. They all stared back at him.

This scene—of dark brown children in ragged
clothes against old adobe walls—was one he had
imagined many times, and now he was actually
here, in the heart of it. He couldn't help feeling

there was something so, well, authentic about it, but he knew that would sound naive to his professors back home. He smiled self-consciously and nodded to the children before turning back to face the gate. On the other side, he could hear Señora Marquez set down a heavy skillet and make her way slowly from the kitchen. The gate swung open and a tiny woman gave him a quizzical look.

"*Perdóname Señora, yo soy Matt Cohen.*" he said in his best college Spanish.

Señora Marquez said nothing and studied him as he nervously continued. He explained that he was sent by Professor Jackson of the University of Michigan Department of Anthropology. Do you remember Professor Jackson? He was here last year and spoke to you about me coming to interview you?

Señora Marquez pursed her lips as she tried to remember. There was a gringo here last year, but she didn't recall his name, and she wasn't clear about what this new gringo wanted, but he seemed to indicate he'd like to come into the courtyard and talk. She beckoned him toward a chair under the tree and closed the gate behind him.

The *casa* of Señora Marquez was well-known to Pablito and his friends, but they had never been inside it, and they stared briefly through the open gate, which was rarely ever open, into the secret courtyard. It was said—some of their aunts had said it—that she was a *bruja* who mixed strange

potions in her kitchen, and they should stay away
from there. Pablito suspected they said those things
to keep kids from going far from home after dark.
But he couldn't be sure, so he always stayed a safe
distance from the *casa de Señora Marquez*. And he
never went down that street after dark.

After the gate closed, Pablito walked on down
the street and turned at the corner, to his job
cleaning Nacho's workshop and helping to build
interesting pieces of furniture. He worked there
every morning and attended school in the
afternoons. There was always lots of fragrant
sawdust on the floor, mingled with those small and
delicate curls that fall from the work of carving and
planing wood. He swept and dusted everything to
start each day, and he mixed it into a pile at the
back fence with dirt and kitchen waste to put on
the garden later in the year. Nacho was a wise man
who believed in using everything.

This morning as he worked, Pablito told Nacho
about the strange gringo in the dirty truck from
Meecheegan. Nacho continued to carve and asked
him to describe the gringo, and he proceeded to
tell about the very light skin, the reddish beard, the
clean bluejeans, the heavy lace-up boots and a
broad-brimmed, khaki-colored sombrero. Pablito
was used to Nacho's endless questions and his
attention to detail so he tried to be thorough.
Sometimes, when Pablito was describing a scene
or event, it seemed as if Nacho had been there
instead of Pablito.

"*¿Era zurdo?*" Nacho asked.

Pablito paused searching for an answer to whether the gringo was left-handed or not, until Nacho smiled and winked and prompted him with another question.

"Which hand did he ring the bell with?" he asked quietly.

"The right one!" grinned Pablito.

"Was he wearing a belt? Tell me about the buckle."

"I didn't see the belt." Pablito admitted defeat. He'd been beaten at this morning's game.

"Ah well. It's probably not an important detail, anyway." said Nacho, "Except that, if it had a big shiny buckle, he's probably a boisterous person."

Pablito thought for a moment that this gringo seemed a little shy and was probably too quiet to be boisterous, and so his buckle was probably not big and shiny.

Pablito returned to work, thinking quietly to himself of these observations and what they might mean. The morning passed quickly, Nacho handed Pablito his usual 20 pesos, and he went off to school. He knew that Nacho didn't really need him to work there, but Nacho believed in education and told Pablito that as long as he stayed in school, he could keep the job. It was a good job, too, that gave him enough money to buy a new book now and then, and an ice cream cone sometimes after school. On the way to school he noticed that the gringo's truck was still parked in front of the *casa de Señora Marquez*.

In the morning, Pablito was surprised to see the gringo's truck parked in front of Nacho's workshop. He entered quietly so as not to disturb the discussion, but Nacho saw him and said, "Ah, this is Pablito, my helper. Pablito, this is Matt Cohen from *Meecheegan*."

Matt Cohen put out his hand and said, "*Mucho gusto en conocerle,*" in a very strange accent.

Pablito smiled shyly and shook the gringo's hand before beginning his duties for the day. Nacho spoke his Spanish slowly and clearly as if he were speaking to a small child so the gringo could understand, and he seemed to be speaking just loud enough for Pablito to hear every word. Pablito felt he was meant to listen closely to the conversation, and so he did.

It was late morning when the gringo thanked Nacho for his time and left in his truck. Nacho began slowly carving the headboard again as Pablito gave him a puzzled look.

"I can see you have many questions." Nacho told his young helper. "That is a good thing."

Pablito asked why he told the gringo those things when he had told Pablito something very different. Nacho continued carving while he spoke.

"I am glad you are so observant, my young friend. Señor Matt Cohen has come a very long ways to study our indigenous culture," he began, "and he should not go away disappointed."

Nacho carefully explained the term "indigenous culture" to his young friend, and Pablito replied, "But you're not from this area originally. You're from Mexico City, aren't you?"

"Yes I am," Nacho replied. "Did you hear me ask what Señora Marquez had told him?"

"Yes, she said that she has seen you often gather shells and seaweed by the full moon," said Pablito, "and that it's an ancient custom of the people because the good energy is concentrated then. She said you return to the house to make magical potions while everyone is asleep. That you have some of the strongest magic in the village and that she knows she's safe as long as you continue to collect the shells and seaweed in the moonlight, just as the old ones did."

"And what did I say to him?" Asked Nacho.

"You told him it was true. That it was indeed the way of the ancients," said Pablito.

"That is all true. And what did I tell you, my friend?"

"You said you go out under the full moon because of the incredible beauty you see there when the light is reflected from the waves. You take a bucket and gather shells and seaweed in the quiet time. You call it 'a gift from the sea.' Then you rinse it well and dig it into the garden for added calcium."

"That is also true." said Nacho.

Pablito was puzzled.

"My young friend, each of us is our own indigenous culture." Nacho continued, "When I studied anthropology at the National University in Mexico City, I collected much data about indigenous peoples and I put it all down on paper. When the stack of paper was thick enough, they filed it away in a large library where it will never be seen again, and told me I was an expert with the right to place important titles after my name. But later in life, I found that much of the information I had gathered was untrue. Although it was not purposefully wrong, it was slanted by individual viewpoints. It did not apply to the entire culture I had spent all that time studying because there are so many different people in each culture doing things in their own way.

"It was then I realized that I had only earned the right to study life perpetually. The more I learned, the less I became an expert on anything. Each question I answer leads to a dozen more. It's all part of the beauty of life, and it's why I enjoy gathering shells in the quiet of a moonlit night when each wave sparkles as it comes to the shore. That's when life is at its most beautiful, and those shells are a gift of magic from the sea when I add them to my garden."

"Shouldn't you have told the gringo that Señora Marquez is wrong?" asked Pablito.

"But Señora Marquez is not wrong, although that's not the way you or I might see it. She is old and needs to believe those things in order to feel safe in her home. Who am I to say she's wrong?"

"But what about the gringo? He'll go away with strange ideas about us!"

"Yes, and he'll put it all down on paper, they'll file it in a large library where nobody will see it, and they'll call him an expert, too," replied Nacho. "But he needs that title to continue in his career, and why should I deny him that?"

Pablito sighed and looked away, deep in thought. Then he returned to sweeping the shop.

***

9

Robert had fond thoughts of most of the guys around town, and the rest he didn't spend much time thinking about at all. A few of his closest friends were buddies who moved down here because Robert had invited them for a stay, and one of them was his hardheaded old high school buddy, Ed Kestler. They hadn't seen each other in close to 40 years, but they finally reconnected just five years ago and now Ed was another one of the expat regulars around Tiburón. It's a beguiling little town that way.

Robert remembered one of their early discussions over beers at a favorite bar in Albuquerque.

***

Ed

Ed swallowed a mouthful of beer and set his glass back in the exact center of the wet ring that glistened on the bar. He turned to Robert.

"So is it safe living down there? I hear a lot of stories about gunfights and kidnappings in Mexico. And crooked cops too. What's the deal, anyway?"

Robert looked over the top of their two beers and said, "Are you effing kidding me? How many mass shooting were there in the US just this week? Grade school kids cut down by sicko classmates who can buy assault weapons and ammo? Random shootings at the local mall? Mass murders at a country music concert in Las Vegas? You actually live in a country where every sick and paranoid person can go buy guns? And you think you're safer here?"

"You're telling me there aren't shootings in Mexico? The news is full of gang wars, with dozens being killed down there."

"Yes, that's all true," said Robert, "but it doesn't affect you. We heard all that stuff, too, after we moved south, so we figured we'd better follow the news and see if we were in danger. And if we were, we'd get the hell out. We're not stupid. But it appears that we and the other expats are not the targets at all. In Mexico the average person can't buy guns, so only the professionals have them. And the Mexican government lets those guys fight out their turf wars as long as they don't target the expats, who are one of the main economic pillars of the country. There are about a million of us down there, but we're not rich enough for anybody to bother kidnapping us because then they'd face the consequences. The drug bosses are quick to deal with those guys who don't follow the rules because they bring unwanted attention to the drug trade and other criminal activities. So yeah, they clean those guys out of society and we feel safe in Mexico."

"OK, fair enough," he said, "This country has gone sick since we were kids. I agree with that. So I go down and visit you in Bahía Tiburón. What the hell is there to do in Bahía Tiburón?"

"Nothin', really." Robert took a sip from his glass and waited for a reaction. Robert had always liked to visit Tony's Tavern when he was north of the border. There were quiet places at Tony's where people could talk, where the TV wasn't too loud. There was an artistic pattern to the overlapping wet rings that his beer glass had created, although it probably annoyed Ed. He loved meeting Ed here at Tony's whenever he got back to the States. And he loved baiting Ed with these pauses.

"Nothin'?" Ed asked in astonishment. "There's nothin' to do, so just come on down and do nothin', right? What kind of a deal is that, Robert? I appreciate the invitation but why do I want to come all the way down there and do nothin'?"

Robert smiled and looked at his beer for a moment. But Ed wasn't finished.

"I mean, what do you and Liz do all day? Just nothin? You just sit and stare at the walls, or what?"

"Not at all, Ed," Robert replied, "We wake up in the morning, have sex, go for a walk and a swim, have breakfast, read a bit, have lunch and do some writing, have some more sex, clean up and go out for dinner, then come back home and have sex, enjoy a nice glass of brandy as we read a good book, and then sleep it off 'til morning."

Ed stared at Robert.

Robert continued, "Next day we just do the same thing, so we don't get confused. We don't want to have to write out a schedule, since we're retired now."

Ed was still staring at Robert. Finally he spoke.

"Ok Robert, now tell me about the bad parts."

"OK, I get it. You and Liz can just hop in the sack anytime you want." Ed said, "What about me? There any nice extra widder–wimmen down there?"

"Sure, there are some nice ladies around town, and most of them are very interesting." Robert said.

"All of em pretty ancient, I suppose."

"There are a few that aren't. And you're not all that young either."

"What if I can't get one of em to play around with me?"

"Then I guess you'll just have to play with yourself."

"That figures." Ed cinched his mouth into a semi-frown. "But hell, that's what I been doin' living in Denver anyway. Can't be any worse down there, can it?"

"We like it." Robert smiled his usual contented smile.

"Must be alright, I guess," said Ed. "You're always sittin' around grinnin' like a possum eatin' grapes." It was one of Ed's favorite Kentuckyisms, and Robert never got tired of any of them. "Must be alright down there, I guess."

"What about football?" Now Ed was getting to the meat of the conversation. "You get cable down there?"

"Yeah. There are people down there with cable."

"Is it hard to get? I mean, how do you do it?"

"Dunno. Never tried," Robert answered. "We just watch the game at a local restaurant. It's a great way to hang out with some of our friends"

"You don't have TV at home? Whatta you do in the evenings for entertainment? Oh wait, you already told me that."

Robert paused and sipped his beer, waiting for Ed's next question.

"What kinda games you watch at the restaurant?"

"You know, *fútbol*."

"Football? American football? In English?"

"Actually, you'd call it soccer."

"Hmm," Ed muttered to his beer, his longtime closest confidant. "Maybe I should go down there sometime and see what this place is all about. I might just learn a new thing or two, even if it harelips th' guvner."

***

And with that kind of attitude, Robert had been pretty sure Ed would make it in Tiburón. Especially after he spent a day or two out fishing in the magical waters of the famous Sea of Cortez.

***

El Viento

Bahía Tiburón was now in the fifth day of a three-day blow. That's how Ed Kestler had it figured. Weather reports weren't considered accurate in this part of the northern Sea of Cortez. Reports from that latest techno marvel, the offshore virtual buoy they installed last year, were also spotty. And conditions along the coast were usually unrelated to the weather inland at Hermosillo, since the Sea is essentially an extension of those giant parallel seismic folds to the north that created Death Valley, Owens

Valley, and the Imperial Valley between the mountains of Southern California. Whenever there's a large low pressure system north of the border spreading snow across the US, heavy cold air drains down those long valleys that lead from the high mountains of the west to the ocean, and it creates *santana* winds that wreak havoc, fanning the annual brush fires that sweep Southern California. The Sea of Cortez is basically the largest of the western valleys, and cold air can pour down across the Sea for days at a time. Until the low pressure system containing all that cold air moves farther east.

Ed had a way of visualizing the big picture and the great interconnectedness of the systems of the world. But Kati Martinez usually thought he was full of hot air. It was one of the many things they seemed to contend over on their occasional dates and forays into a relationship that had developed after Ed got to Tiburón. Ed had once remarked that the dolphins that swam along the beach about once a week usually seemed to come from the east. Kati saw them coming from the west once, and that also became a topic of discussion. Ed had not said they "always" came from the east, but that's how Kati heard it. Or that's how she wanted to interpret what Ed said, and really, that's all that mattered.

But it had been blowing long enough that Ed was ready for a change. He sometimes checked the weather reports from Yuma, Arizona, which was upwind—up the long valley, from Bahía Tiburón—to see what the wind forecast would be. It wasn't always 100%, but it generally gave him a reasonable idea of what to expect. The report showed another day of wind for Yuma, so Ed resigned himself to it. The wind was gonna do what the wind was gonna do. That's how the cards were dealt. You had to play with what you got, and sometimes you lost your ante. Too bad.

He liked a good card-playing metaphor even though he thought poker was boring. A well-timed reference to card playing usually came in handy when he had to deal with some of the worst hard-case right-wingers in town. "Far-right wing-nuts," he called them. It was one of the things he and Kati agreed on. A good poker reference came in handy to inoculate him against some of the harder characters around town. But sometimes it got him invited to a poker game, which he considered to be a boring way to spend an afternoon, and usually, lose some money. The prospect of getting trapped into a game that some of these guys had studied all their lives reminded him of another appropriate saying: "If you're invited to a poker game and you don't know who the designated sucker is, it's probably you."

Ed was of two minds about the wind. As an old sailor, he understood the interplay of the differential in temperatures between the land and the Sea, and how that dictated the movements of that great air mass we call "the wind." He understood it and he appreciated its power and its importance as a weather regulator on a global scale. But when it lasted this long, the wind just got annoying. He decided to call Fred Johnson, his occasional fishing buddy, to see if he wanted to go to *El Pulpo Verde* to get a beer and a plate of steamed clams while they commiserated over the weather. He knew that Fred was going stir-crazy by now because he couldn't launch his fishing boat. And it's true, he reflected, that misery loves company.

When Ed entered the *Pulpo*, a strong gust of wind rearranged all the napkin settings on the nearest table before he got the door closed. Ed felt a little embarrassed, but Francisco, one of the waiters, walked over and put everything back in order in plenty of time for the next customer to open the door and blow things back into disarray. Chuy was playing his guitar on the little bandstand in the corner. Ed had forgotten that Chuy played every Friday afternoon and then late into the evening. Chuy was a good guitar player, but a couple of years ago he'd bought an electric guitar and an amp so people could hear him above all the conversation. The electrification of music in the restaurants of Mexico was a trend that Ed had not appreciated. It made conversation difficult for someone with a low voice, like Ed. Especially since Fred wore hearing aids. Sometimes Ed ended up hoarse after shouting at Fred over lunch.

Ed had no way to contact Fred to suggest a change of plans, so he ordered a cold Bohemia and resigned himself to living with the din. He and Fred didn't have anything important to talk about, anyway. They were both bachelors who just wanted to get out of the house.

As Fred walked through the door, the wind rearranged the table settings again, but Fred did not seem to notice. Chuy was singing, "Winna wussa lil bi bebe mai mama wua rok mey inna creyel inem ol con fils bey kom."

"What the hell is he singing now?" asked Fred. "Is he butchering 'Cotton Fields' again? Why doesn't he learn the words? That sounds ridiculous!"

"Fred, relax," Ed said. "Who really cares, anyway? It's just background noise. You know Chuy doesn't speak English. He's just mouthing the words to the song."

"You're right he doesn't speak English!" said Fred, who tended to let some things get to him. "You should have seen what happened when he did that tile work for me! I did my best to communicate with him and left to go in to Hermosillo for more materials. He got the pattern all backwards! What a mess!"

Ed had to suppress a laugh. He remembered the incident, and Fred's histrionic reaction.

"Oh Fred, it wasn't that bad," he offered. It seemed that Ed spent the beginning of every conversation unruffling Fred's feathers. "You make a big deal out of these things. I thought it looked kind of creative. In fact, I thought it made you look like a creative genius."

Fred was used to Ed's blowing smoke up his ass. "Creative genius, hell!" he replied. "You're always covering for the Mexicans when they screw something up! If they want to work for me they oughta learn some English!"

"Wait a minute, Fred!" Ed laughed. They'd been down this road many times before. "This is their country, isn't it? Don't you think you should learn a little Spanish?"

Fred gave a rueful half smile because he knew he was sounding ridiculous. In fact, when a crew full of Mexican immigrants came to work at Fred's other house in Denver he always carped about how they should speak English in the US. And yes,

Ed had often reminded him about his
double standard.

"Sure it's their damn country, and they
don't hafta learn English if they don't wanta.
But if they wanna work for me you'd think
they'd learn how to talk to me. I mean I've
got the money, and they want the job, right?"

Fred was starting to calm down now.
This was how it always worked. He spent a
lot of time in that little house of his, and
things tended to build up when he didn't
have an outlet for it. He just needed to
relieve the pressure. Especially in this
endless wind.

"But really, Ed, you know I took those
Spanish classes they gave at the Club. I really
did try to learn the language, but it just
doesn't come easy for me, like it does for
you. Hey, what's going on with that damn
wind? Look at it out there blowing the palm
trees around. Is it ever gonna stop? It's been
blowing since they invented tortillas!"

Their talks always had abrupt turns, and
whiplash was a hazard in a conversation
with Fred.

Spanish hadn't come easy for Ed, either,
but he kept trying to use it anytime he went to
the little *tienda* on the corner, where the nice
lady at the cash register sometimes giggled at
his attempts, and whenever he ordered dinner
out. And slowly, Ed started to sound like he

might be getting it. But Spanish was still a major struggle for him.

About twice a week Ed would pick up a copy of the local newspaper and translate a few stories. It was good way to learn Spanish and to stay up with the local news. And Ed had the other advantage of hanging out with Kati, who could help him out with the more difficult passages.

Her actual name was Catarina Martinez. She had long dark hair and sparkling eyes and she was born in Mexico City, so she spoke Spanish fluently. Ed called her a *dictionario de pelo largo,* his long-haired dictionary.

And not only did Kati speak Spanish fluently, but she also spoke it clearly and not like many of the local people who spoke a difficult and slangy version that Ed called *sonorense.* Ed had wondered if moving south of the border would help him find a nice lady to hang out with and he'd been amazed, mostly at himself, to find that this smart Mexican beauty thought him worthy of redemption. Few of the ladies north of the border had seemed to notice the special qualities she apparently saw in him.

Ed still wasn't sure what she saw through those big gorgeous eyes, but he decided not to mess this opportunity up if he could help it. Not like all those other opportunities in the past. He reflected that maybe he was finally growing up, treating her with decency and respect, and putting all those stupid boyhood ideas behind him.

And Kati had taught Ed a few *dichos*, or sayings, in Spanish. They came in handy now and then and made Ed look like he knew a lot more Spanish than he did. So now he shared one with Fred.

"You know Fred, in any country people have trouble with their workers, and in Spanish they say, *'El quien paga, manda.'* It means, 'The guy who pays makes the rules.'"

"Oh. Just like the 'golden rule,' huh?" said Fred. "The guy with the gold makes the rules."

"Yeah. Pretty much the same thing," said Ed. "But you'd still make your life a lot easier here if you learned a bit more Spanish."

Over the years Ed realized there was a lot more to living in Mexico, and in a good way, than he'd ever thought of. It was the little things that made the biggest difference. After a few years in town people would say *"Buenos Dias, Señor Ed."* when they passed on the street. He was referred to now as *"Caballero"* by the waiters at Casa Serena, which had become his favorite hangout with friends for a good lunch or dinner. It was a lot better than being "old and in the way," like in that bluegrass song.

And he noticed the impression he made when leaving a restaurant by simply saying *"Con permiso,"* as he passed a Mexican family enjoying their dinner. They were surprised when a gringo even knew of that traditional politeness, that bit of old-fashioned charm. And it made him appear to be a true *caballero*.

As they stepped outside Fred said, "You know Ed, you're looking more, um, prosperous these days."

Ed laughed and said, "You mean fat, right? I can't help it because Kati cooks up such healthy meals and I don't have to eat canned beans anymore. She's been a real gift that I hadn't expected and probably don't deserve."

Fred nodded and said, "Now there's a good reason to learn Spanish."

The wind seemed to reach a peak much later during the night as it shrieked through the palms outside Fred's bedroom window and rattled a loose piece of roofing that he swore he was going to repair if the wind ever quit. But the wind did quit sometime during the night, and the Sea looked glassy and beautiful in the morning. But Fred never could find that loose piece of roofing after the wind stopped blowing.

So Fred called Ed and said, "You ready for some fishing?"

***

10

There was something about the way they did things in Mexico that often caught Robert by surprise. No matter how long he lived in this curious culture, he was frequently caught wrong-footed by some new or ridiculous development that he could never foresee. But then it would seem to make perfect sense when he stopped to look at it from the Mexican point of view.

The community was glad when the local internet guys appeared along the street to string up new fiber optic cables on the old telephone poles. The local internet service had been agonizingly slow at times, on top of the usual world wide wait, and this new technology promised to give the system a real boost.

The crew did a quick job of stringing the lines and all would soon be better, he hoped, than it ever had been before, after everything was connected. And as the lines were strung, the crews stapled a bright yellow sign on each post that wrapped around it to tell the local copper thieves that there was no copper in these lines, in hopes they wouldn't climb up there and cut into it just to check.

The sign read *"No contiene cobre,"* in large letters, so everyone could read it. But the signs were wider than the circumference of the poles, and as each sign wrapped around, it covered the first part of the notice so the thieves could only read, *"contiene cobre."*

Robert snorted when he noticed the mis-installed yellow signs on poles near his house. Then he shook his head as he wandered back inside, and he mumbled *"¡Así es Méjico!"*

***

Las Vacas Priistas
(The PRI-ista Cows)

"What the hell!?!"

Ed Kestler had been driving very slowly, probably less than 10 mph, into one of those dense night fogs that settle over Bahía Tiburónes now and then. It wasn't possible to see much farther than the front of the car. He was on his way back from a big meal and a *margarita grande* with friends, and he suddenly slammed on the brakes because he was sure there was something—he did not know what, a shape or something—in the road just ahead of his front bumper. As he stared into the white cloud of fog reflecting the glare of his headlights, he finally saw two enormous dull eyes staring back at him.

He knew he hadn't had so much to drink that he was hallucinating, and anyway he was driving very slowly, only creeping along, just in case. He knew his reactions were not as razor-sharp as when he was younger, and his eye sight was also not as sharp, on top of that grande-sized margarita. And there were almost no other cars on the road—yet another one of the reasons he liked this small village by the Sea of Cortez. On any average weeknight like this one, there was an almost complete lack of nightlife, and no traffic. Enjoying an extra drink was a frequent option. Most nights you could just walk down the middle of the deserted street to get home. And walking in the street was generally safer than walking on the broken sidewalks in almost any Mexican town. As he'd gotten older he'd come to appreciate these simple pleasures. But he hadn't counted on this dense fog dropping over the town while he was inside that restaurant at the far end of town with a table full of friends.

Yet now he was staring intently into two large and stupid-looking eyes as they slowly blinked back at him. Then he gradually made out the shape of a very large black cow standing in the middle of the road. He realized his jaw was hanging open and he felt like some kind of caricature, a cartoon figure almost. He closed his mouth and swallowed hard and realized he was short of breath. He felt his heart racing and he loosened his grip on the wheel. He took a few deep breaths, dropped his shoulders, exhaled hard, and sat back in the seat, while the cow stood there and stared back at him. Slowly he eased the car forward until his bumper tapped the cow who jumped slightly before thudding off the road with heavy footsteps. Then the cow stood on the broken sidewalk and stared as Ed slowly eased past. To his left he now saw another cow, mostly white. Another cow, mostly black, was standing with the white one. They all stared in their stupid way as he eased past.

"Why the black one?!" he shouted, to nobody in particular, since he was alone in the car. "Why not the white one? Why wasn't that white one standing in the road, instead of the black one!?! In the fog!?! I could have run into the damn thing!!"

Ed thought about all the things in life that were mostly caused by luck, usually bad luck. He was sure there were quite a few twists in history that were the result of blind luck or stupidity instead of heroism. He would think more about that in the morning when he could maybe recall a few examples, but that would be tomorrow in the clear light of day after the drink had worn off and the fog had lifted. For now, he was amused by how much more philosophical and deeply intelligent he usually felt after a stiff drink or two.

Then he muttered, "Goddam Lalo Moreno and his goddam PRI-ista cows."

Lalo Moreno grew up in the countryside on a hardscrabble farm near Tiburón. He was a proud

son of rural Sonora, where the earliest stirrings of
the Revolution began a hundred years ago, and
where Plutarco Elias Calles, the founder of the
PRI was from. Like most Mexicans, Lalo
identified more with his native state than with
those *chilangos* down in Mexico City who stole
the taxes he paid, although he hardly ever paid
any taxes. And they looted the treasury. That's
why the roads were always crumbling here in
Sonora, and probably everywhere else in the
country, as far as he knew. The water was unsafe
to drink and the electricity was always on the
blink. And now the PAN, the hated right-
wingers, were back in power and he knew
they'd return the country to the old feudal days
of mass peonage and repression under the boot-
heel of the Church. Did those brave miners suffer
and die for nothing in the rebellion at Cananea
that started the great Revolution? Did Emiliano
Zapata die for nothing in that betrayal at the
Hacienda de San Juan? Was the great legacy of
Presidente Lázaro Cárdenas to be sold for a few
pieces of silver?

That's how Lalo Moreno saw it. He was
devoted to the battle, to *la lucha,* over moral
principles. His cows were a symbol of a
righteous cause. He had little use for Eduardo
Encinas, the newly appointed PAN-ista alcalde
of Tiburón. And Eduardo had little use for Lalo.

It was Eduardo who had already issued
several citations against Lalo's cows because he

refused to keep them penned up and off the
streets and public sidewalks. Lalo had ignored
all the citations, and even burned one publicly at
a PRI rally in the town plaza.

Ed knew Lalo well enough. His wife cooked
up the best tamales in town, and Ed made a
habit of getting half a dozen every Thursday,
before the weekend crowds arrived to enjoy the
beach. He could relate to Lalo's hardscrabble
upbringing, even if Lalo regarded him as just
another one of those gringos who had taken
away half of Mexico in that war long ago. Sure,
his family needed the gringo's money, but he
wasn't about to admit it.

He was also the guy who backed into Ed's
car once and left a big dent in the driver's door.
And then he drove off. And when Ed returned
and saw that smear of dirty purple paint on the
dent he knew it had been Lalo, but so what? Lalo
had no money and he wasn't going to pay for the
repairs. On the positive side, at least now Ed's
truck blended in better with most of the other
vehicles around Tiburón.

Ed really didn't have a lot of options in
dealing with that dent. After he moved south of
the border a few years ago he learned that
nobody ever contacted the *policia* for something
this minor, because nothing good ever comes out
of dealing with the *policia*. And by now he also
knew that Mexico was a country ruled by pride
and an extreme version of libertarianism mingled

with fatalism. He took a deep breath, shrugged his shoulders, and accepted that at least now the car was less likely to be stolen. You needed a good sense of humor to make it here, even if it hurt. The dictator Porfirio Diaz was probably right long ago when he told the people who ousted him that they had no idea what forces they were about to release as the country's bloody *Revolución* began.

And Ed also knew Eduardo, the PAN-ista *Alcalde* and wealthy owner of the local Pemex franchise, where the pumps where rigged.

As the party that represents the merchant class, the new PAN regime had a mission to clean up Tiburón to make it more attractive as a tourist destination. Several local store owners complained that the ridiculous sight of cattle in the street and wandering down the sidewalk made the town look like some backwoods cow pasture. And they left big cow pies on the sidewalks that never got cleaned up. It wasn't an image the PAN and the local shopkeepers wanted to promote. In their eyes, Lalo was making them and the new *alcalde* look like fools. So Eduardo finally had the cows arrested as a public hazard and placed in a corral at the edge of town.

After the cows were detained, Lalo went into Hermosillo and talked to his cousin who had grown up with the new PAN-ista *Presidente* of Hermosillo, the man who had appointed

Eduardo to be the *alcalde* of Tiburón, and he got the cows released. In Sonora, familial and fraternal bonds remain strong, regardless of party affiliation. But Lalo still made no provisions to fence in his cows, and he turned them loose again to wander as they pleased. Just like before.

Complaints soon mounted again, and Eduardo organized *vaqueros* and several large trucks to round up the cows again and haul them to an impound lot on the far side of Hermosillo, about 80 miles away. That appeared to be the end of it, because the cows were worth less than the cost of transporting them back to Tiburón. But within two weeks, the PRI-ista cows were back. On the same trucks. And they'd been well-fed at the government's expense. Their transportation was paid for, some said, by the Governor's office, a post that was currently occupied by a PRI-ista.

So Eduardo gave up and moved on to more important issues and more pressing needs for the small quiet town nestled by the Sea of Cortez. And Lalo's cows, now considered to be local PRI-ista heroes, went back to crapping on the sidewalks of Tiburón. And appearing suddenly, in the fog.

***

11

It was getting late as Robert finally closed the big binder of loose-leaf pages he'd been looking over, the latest rough cut of a maybe-someday book that never seemed to get completed, and he took another sip from the glass of brandy sitting on the shelf beside him. His stories were now peppered with Liz's notes. She was a brutal critic, and sometimes it was just plain annoying. But she was also often right. And now it looked, at least to her, like he just might have a book worth wrapping up. If he would just get the thing finished.

The November evening air was a bit cool, and Robert rose from his easy chair to close the door to the seaside veranda and turn on that electric fireplace insert he'd bought over the internet for a couple hundred dollars. It was kind of tacky in its own way, but it made the living room feel warm and welcoming—which the expensive gas insert that it replaced had never managed to do. That damn thing just smoked up the glass doors and there seemed to be no way to get it adjusted right. And the electric unit put out just as much heat.

The winter weather was another odd thing about Bahía Tiburón. It was far enough north that it had real seasons. People think that if you live on a beach in Mexico it's always warm and tropical. Robert enjoyed those long warm months when he could hang out in his *gorra, gafas, playera, chortes, y chanclas* and watch the waves go by. Soon enough he'd be wearing long pants again, and close-toed shoes. "Close-toads" he called them, and he wasn't looking forward to it.

In Tiburón the winters can be windy and chilly, especially for folks who have managed to avoid seeing snow for several decades. That makes for lots of time inside to work on the next chapter of a book. And maybe finish a novella that just might find a good place at the end of whatever book he ended up with.

It was a larger tale about life here in Tiburón, but it also involved a tragic local event that had bothered Robert for several years. And now he wanted to put those thoughts to rest.

A Novella

El Charrito

ector Salido Moreno was born to the Sea. Most of the young men born in Bahía Tiburón had gone to sea at an early age with their fathers, or maybe with an uncle. In Hector's case, it was his Tio Alfredo who recognized a certain fire in the eyes of this newborn, and he believed that a male child born in Tiburón was surely destined to go to sea. This child was born in November on the day of San Andrés, the patron saint of fishermen. So Alfredo convinced Padre Felipe, who also understood the ways of the Sea, to baptize the boy on the town beach, in the salty waters of the Sea of Cortez.

It was a chilly morning in January, and the Sonoran coast was swept by one of those four-day winds that pour down at that time of the year from snowy mountains north of the border. A group of aunts, uncles, and cousins had assembled in the cold as waves brushed the shore, angling in from the northwest. There was a light layer of cloud in the sky that blocked most of the sun's warming rays. Hector's mother, Lupita, had the boy bundled in an old blanket, wrapped tightly against the clawing wind.

Hector's father, a mason and plasterer, was working in Guerrero Negro, a tough saltworks town on the Pacific coast of the Baja, and had not yet seen the child. Lupita put the swaddled baby into the rough hands of Tio Alfredo, who patiently waited as the cold water lapped his legs to where his coarse brown trousers were tightly rolled above his knees. The Padre, standing beside him in the cold water, solemnly read the service. At the moment of baptism, Tio Alfredo unwrapped the child and gave the naked boy to the Padre who dipped him into the cold water. The child stared into the Padre's eyes and listened to his droning voice as the cold water enveloped him. Lupita was surprised when Hector made no cry of alarm— no sound at all, and that's when Tio Alfredo knew that the boy was truly destined for the Sea.

Back in those days Tiburón was a small village of about 20 families who lived off the bounteous ocean. The surrounding land was nothing but forbidding desert— forbidding and unforgiving. But the Sea was abundant with fish and provided food for the village, and enough for export to the big city of Hermosillo. The nearby estuary produced tiny clams, crabs, shrimp, and vast schools of *sardinas* that left its protection as they grew larger to skim the shores of the open Sea hungrily searching for smaller prey. And in their own season, bands of large migratory fish swept through, feeding on the schools of little silvery fish. Clouds of hungry birds, *pelícanos, gaviotas* and high-flying *tijeretas* also plundered the small fish in savage diving attacks, falling hungrily and recklessly on them by the hundreds when they migrated through each year in the

Spring and again in the Fall, following one of the most important flyways of the world.

Summers were long and suffocatingly hot, and the winters along the northern coastal desert could be bitterly cold for a few weeks each year when north winds from the California Sierra poured down the Sea to build treacherous waves that pounded the shore through the night. That's when the thunder of large crashing waves rocked the shacks of the small town and made it hard to sleep, as if the angry ancient gods of the Sea had returned to remind the villagers of their power. Lupita huddled with tiny Hector and made the sign of the cross through those long cold nights as their crude little shack creaked and twisted in the savage winds. And she hoped that hers would not be one of the fragile and flammable hovels that burned each year from unattended fires, taking precious lives with them.

Sometimes, during those long days and nights of wind, a panga would be caught out at the islands and those aboard had no choice but to wait until the Sea became less angry. *Pescadores* who were caught out in the windy season pulled their boats onto rocky beaches among the distant islands and waited as the winds lashed their rude encampment, filling their eyes and mouths with dust. They built small fires for cooking, and they waited, and they watched, with the endless patience of the poor, as white-capped waves marched endlessly southward. The women of the village went to the simple adobe *iglesia* by the dusty plaza and prayed for their men to return. Mostly, God showed his mercy, and the men returned to their families. But sometimes the Sea took them away without a trace.

Alfredo Coronado Salido had been a fisherman, a
pescador, for all his life. He didn't know exactly when he
began fishing with his own father and his uncles as a
small child, but he could not remember ever not being a
fisherman. When he turned 18 he earned enough money
to buy his own boat, an older panga that was still good
and strong, and he called her *La Guadalupana*, after his
patron saint. And when he had enough money, he bought
a larger motor so he could go farther out where the fishing
was better. Now these many years later, after baptizing his
tiny *sobrino* in the cold water, he looked forward to the
day when he would take Hector with him.

The day after Hector turned three years old, Tio Alfredo
took him out to fish the large ocean, along with Juan
and Rubén, two of Hector's older cousins. Alfredo
remembered that trip, and little Hector watching closely
as he and the cousins crossed themselves and muttered a
prayer before heading off shore, and later while they
baited hooks and checked crab traps. Tio Alfredo pulled in
his lines, and Hector's eyes grew wide when he saw big
silvery fish attached to the hooks and the colorful ancient-
looking crabs, *cangrejos,* that came up in their crude wire
traps. The boy was fascinated by everything that had to do
with the ocean, and he seemed to stare at the mysterious
and magical surface of the water for the information that
led his Tio Alfredo to the wondrous creatures below.

As he grew older, Hector became a regular part of the
crew on *La Guadalupana* and within a few years was
catching his own share of the rich bounty offered by the
Sea. When Hector was ten years old, his cousin Juan left

the boat to try crossing the border to *el otro lado,* the other side. Alfredo had known for many years that Juan was a bright and ambitious boy, and not really meant for a life at sea. Juan had married Marú, a beautiful local girl, when he turned 19 and was now the father of twin girls who were growing quickly and would soon start primary school. He wanted to provide better for his family than a life on the margins of the Sea could allow. He no longer wanted his family to live in a tarpaper shack with no running water and two bare bulbs hanging from wires.

Alfredo was sad to see one of his *sobrinos* leave the village and *La Guadalupana*, but he understood. He also knew how difficult it would be to cross *la linea* into Arizona and walk through the terrible desert to reach Tucson or Phoenix to find a job on a construction site, or in a restaurant, or on a landscaping crew. It was only the hard working jobs that were open to Mexicans, but that was OK. Mexicans still knew how to work hard, a way of life the gringos had forgotten. A year earlier, Alfredo went with his brother Miguel to the Hermosillo bus station to pick up their friend Pedro, who was returning from the north, and he'd seen posters taped to the windows warning young Mexicans about the dangers of crossing the border in the desert. There were several different posters showing various entry points used by the *coyotes* who took people across, and how many days of walking through the waterless desert were required to reach a city, like Tucson. They were also sprinkled with red dots marking each place where someone had died along the way.

Alfredo hadn't really thought of it in those terms before, and he was saddened that so many of his countrymen had perished under the burning sun so far from their villages. There were only a few men from Tiburónes who had crossed the border and they said it was tougher than they'd imagined. They'd spent weeks in Altar, not far from the border, waiting for the chance to cross. There were were rows of small cheap rooms for rent to the border crossers, the *cruceros,* as they waited. *Cruceros* were one of the main businesses in Altar. But the money these men could make on the other side—about ten times what they could make in their villages back home—was worth the risk.

Every one of the *cruceros* that Alfredo had known personally had been successful in crossing. Still, he'd heard about others, even some from the village, who had never been heard from again. He knew it was dangerous. But he knew it was not possible to convince Juan to not go. He only advised him to cross in the Springtime or the Fall when the daytime temperatures were lower but the nights were not freezing cold. Better in the Fall because at that time of the year, there might also be rain showers to leave ponds of drinking water along the way.

Hector cried when he gave Juan a final *abrazo,* as Juan wrapped his two strong arms around his little cousin. Each of them knew it might be the last hug they would ever share. Alfredo looked grim as he turned to ready the boat for another day on the Sea. Juan helped them shove the heavy boat into the water, and then he turned away. Dawn was just breaking over the village. Hector leaned on the gunwales of the panga and watched his cousin Juan as he walked away from the shore to catch the 6:00 am bus. He knew Juan would be gone when they returned from the Sea that afternoon.

It had been a good morning, and they caught a heavy load of fish before returning to the village. Now came the job of unloading the catch and collecting their money from the buyers waiting to haul them away. Hector looked up from lifting fish out of the panga and saw a family of dolphins swimming by just off shore. He turned back to the heavy load of fish they'd brought in, and they were back before the waves started growing large—usually in the late morning, as the on-shore breeze started to build. Tio Alfredo had shown him the ways of the Sea, how the winds built as the sun heated the land, and then tapered off toward sunset. He'd also learned about the night breezes that poured back from the desert and out onto the water in the darkness as the land cooled. Tio Alfredo used this knowledge in the very early morning as he hugged the shore with his panga to stay clear of the larger waves further out. Tio Alfredo never really said much about fishing or the Sea, but he seemed to teach it in a quiet way.

Hector looked up again to watch the dolphins.

"Why do they always swim from the east to the west along the shore?" he asked.

Tio Alfredo glanced at the dolphins, and once again he quietly admired their sleek and efficient bodies. They were purpose-built to live in the Sea, and to catch fish. He had a great deal of respect for such fellow fishermen.

"How do you know they always swim from east to west?" he asked as he resumed unloading the fish.

"Well, I'm not sure, but every time I see them along the shore here, they're heading west."

"Why do you think they would be swimming west along the shore?" he asked.

Tio Alfredo had a way of turning Hector's questions into more questions. Sometimes Hector just wished his uncle would answer the question, and not force him to think about it.

"I don't know," he sighed and went back to unloading the fish.

"What time of day is it?" his Tio asked as he shifted the nets to expose the fish below.

Hector looked around. He squinted toward the sun and he saw narrowing shadows on the west sides of nearby buildings. Other fishermen who had already unloaded their fish were sitting in the shadows, leaning against the walls.

"I don't know," he said. "It's late in the morning, I guess."

"And where is the sun?"

"Still in the east."

"And why do you think the dolphins would swim away from the sun?"

Hector narrowed his eyes and looked into the east.

"So they wouldn't be blinded by the sun?" Hector said and shrugged his shoulders, as youngsters do when they're not sure of an answer and they don't want to look like they've actually committed themselves to one.

"Why's that?" his Tio asked as he continued unloading the fish.

Sometimes his uncle's questions were relentless, and sometimes they left Hector feeling exhausted. Hector took a deep breath and thought for a moment before answering, "So they can see their prey better?"

"And what does the prey see?"

"They're blinded by the sun and can't escape the dolphins," he said as he gazed back at the rapidly disappearing dolphins. Their smooth shiny backs glistened in the late morning each time they broke the surface.

"Hand me the rest of those fish," said Tio Alfredo. "We have to get them to the mercado."

The day's lesson was over.

The *pescadores* of Tiburón caught fish all through the year and sold them to the men with battered old trucks who packed them in ice and hauled the catch on rough dirt roads to distant Hermosillo. There was always enough fish —or squid, or crabs, or clams—for dinner. And there was enough left to trade with the men who worked inland on the farms and brought sacks of the spotted and blemished crops that had been left in the fields after the first and second pickings were finished for the markets north of the border. But the fishermen earned little from selling their catch—just enough to buy second-hand clothing or to pay for a baptism. Now and then, there would be enough left over for candy for the kids. Mostly, though, the kids contented themselves with the sweet seeds that appeared in early summer on the tall shady *guamúchiles,* the trees that grew by their palm thatch huts.

As he got older, the fishbuyers' trucks got newer and fancier. Hector noticed how well dressed the buyers were now, how shiny their boots were in the desert sun, while he and the other fishermen loaded the trucks wearing rags

and worn out shoes or sandals. Those large boats in the
fishing fleet from Guaymas kept the prices low as they
brought up tons of fish in their huge nets. Hector could
see that he and his compadres were barely making enough
to buy fuel for the boat. He began to feel the deep bitterness
of the older fishermen. It made him realize for the first time
that the world, his world, was divided into very different
classes of people. Something about the bitterness troubled
him and seemed sinful. It reminded him of that lesson
from the Bible about eating from the tree of knowledge.
He began to feel a kind of anger deep in his *alma*, his
soul, and he wondered if his anger was somehow a sin.

Like many of the other families, Hector's had come
here from the south, from the jungle-covered hills of
Guerrero. His parents spoke Nahuatl as their first
language, and just enough Spanish to survive in the north
of Mexico. They left Guerrero because there wasn't
enough land for everyone. Hector remembered his parents
telling of bitter times after the terrible bloodshed of the
Revolution. Of men standing silently on broken street
corners in worn and dirty serapes and large straw sombreros,
waiting for work. It was backbreaking work in the fields
that paid no more than a peso a day. Even after Presidente
Cárdenas began fulfilling the promises of the great
revolutionary, Emiliano Zapata, and started to give land to
the people, there was not enough for everyone. And now
he and his family were living far from Guerrero and
working harder than ever, and they still lived in poverty.

His Tio Alfredo dealt with the buyers for Hector's
share of the catch, because they were unnerved by
Hector's angry stares.

Over the years, Hector grew into a fine and strong young man, not one to take an insult from anyone. The hard work of the Sea left him with hardened muscles and an athletic build. His neighbors said he was *toroso,* strong like a little bull. Some called him *torito.* Others called him *charrito,* because he could be unruly and was often in trouble, and maybe too quick to deliver a hard mocking backhand, a *torniscón,* to the face of anyone he felt had insulted him. But after working on the pangas and leaving each morning before dawn, he often came back so tired that he had little energy left for fighting. His Tio Alfredo had watched him closely over the years and he knew the boy could be trouble. Alfredo was a strong man himself with no need to show his power to others. He led by example and seldom said anything bad to the boy, but he seemed to do his best to bring him back exhausted each day.

Saturday nights were different. It didn't matter how hard the men worked, there was usually time enough for a Saturday afternoon *siesta* after they finished work so they'd have enough energy for the weekly *fiesta* and *baile* in the plaza. And sometimes there would be trouble. At times, Hector thought that God even seemed to will it to be, so there would be sins to confess on Sunday morning after mass. But on this Saturday night, there was good reason for celebration. Hector's cousin Juan had returned after six years of work on the other side of the border.

Hector and Rubén had met Juan at the local *parada.* As he swung down from the bus, wearing new jeans, a bright new shirt, and polished boots, they embraced him in heartfelt abrazos. He had written letters to the family, and sent money to his aging parents, Alberto and Maria, but this was the first time he'd been able to return. Hector remembered Juan's dark hair and his handsome smile, and a tear of gratitude came to his eyes. He crossed himself and muttered a "thank you" to his God. The cousins each shouldered a heavy bag and walked to Alberto and Maria's house where the rest of the family was waiting.

It was Don Abelardo Salazar Garcia who brought the huge snorting and rusty machine to Bahía Tiburón on that bright day in the Springtime of Hector's 24th year. He said it was an *empujadora niveladora,* a pushing and leveling machine, to make the work of sculpting the land easier. Don Abelardo said the gringos on the other side of the border called the big machine a bulldozer. Hector liked the sound of that—like a *toro,* a bull—and he liked the deep throated rumble of the machine. He practiced saying bulldozer until he got it right. Without too much accent.

Don Abelardo had plans to create some home sites by the Sea to sell to people from Hermosillo. And maybe to visiting gringos. He planned to blade a road through the dunes just back from the shore, measure off each piece of land, and mark each one with a small wooden sign. He even had a hefty gringo operator named Max to run the big machine. Hector was growing tired of fishing and decided to work for Don Abelardo until the work ran out. He could always go back to fishing later. His Tio Alfredo was sorry to see him leave the fishing life, but he knew it was time, and he was glad his nephew wasn't planning to cross the border.

Hector studied this new gringo in town, Max, and remembered the first time he ever saw a gringo. He was about 10 years old when a large strange boat came to their village and anchored just offshore. It was completely unlike the rough wooden boats that some of his people still poled along the coast in those days, and it had sailed to the rich fishing grounds by the Island. He had never seen a boat like it before, gleaming white and beautiful on the water. He and his friends dragged discarded fish-packing crates into the water, then paddled their old crates out to see the boat and the strange white people aboard. He recalled the people pointing and laughing as he and his amigos paddled toward them. He felt ashamed, but he wasn't sure why. He only knew they were laughing at him.

But this new gringo in town, this guy the Mexicans called "Mahks" was different. He was a rough-hewn, good-natured character who hardly spoke any Spanish. But he could fix anything that broke on the big machine, along with the two graders and the other pieces of heavy equipment he was now in charge of. Hector was assigned to work as his helper.

The bulldozer was old and heavily used—a lot like Max—and it needed plenty of maintenance. Don Abelardo, *el jefe,* had bought it cheap in southern Arizona after it sat unused in the desert for a couple of years—another casualty of the Sun Belt boom in the 1960s and '70s when the Rust Belt collapsed and the best jobs went overseas.

The first thing Max did was remove the old battery cables and repair them to avoid future problems. He soldered the ends on because those old crimped ends had developed an internal corrosion that impeded the flow of

electricity from recharging the batteries. Hector was
surprised that he didn't just put on new cables like the
other gringos did.

"Naw, there's nothing wrong with these cables," said
Max, "and now they're actually better than they were new.
Now they'll work forever."

Max sometimes reminded Hector of his uncle Alfredo.
They came from vastly different cultures, but they both
had the same kind of native wisdom. Hector learned
quickly from the big gringo, and Max appreciated the way
his young Mexican helper could solve problems and repair
things without waiting around for parts to arrive. Parts that
would probably never arrive this far south of the border.

Max was amused when the kid used some old wire to
tie the air filter back together after the sea breeze had
rusted away a couple of bolts. He recalled the many times
he'd done something like that to keep a machine running
so he could finish a job and get paid. He'd fix it the right
way later when he had the cash. Soon Hector was doing
everything to care for the big machine they called *la
bestia,* The Beast, and even operating it to clear lots
while Max was on the big yellow road grader that soon
became another part of Don Abelardo's fleet of older
heavy equipment.

"Ya know Hector, yer lucky," Max said on a blistering
day in summer.

Hector looked quizzically up from changing the oil in
The Beast. He'd never heard a gringo say anything like
that before.

"Yeah, you get a nice tan out here in the sun, but I just
get blistered. Us Irish don't really have the skin tone for

this country. We're so white we have to run whenever we
see Colonel Sanders coming, cause he's always lookin fer
more white meat!"

Hector had seen a Kentucky Fried Chicken place in
Hermosillo once, so he got the reference, and he laughed
along at the joke. Max often said stuff like that, and he
explained it when Hector did not understand. And his
terrible Spanish always made it even funnier. He was a fun
guy to work with and Hector learned a lot from him.

One day Max even shared an insight into why he
was working in Mexico and not making better wages up
north. He'd been a farmer with a small spread in
Oklahoma, and one spring morning he went to the Feed
'n' Seed store in town to get seed for his next crop. He
was working the field when the owner of the Feed 'n'
Seed showed up to tell him the check had bounced. He
went to the bank in town and found out his wife had
come in early to clean out the account and then she'd
run off with a guy she'd met just a few days earlier. Over
the next few weeks Max had to sell off his equipment to
pay the bank, and he was going to lose the farm, when
his wife called on the telephone. She was crying and told
him her new boyfriend had split with the money. She
was really sorry and would Max come down to Texas
and pick her up?

"'Hoowee!' I said, 'I wouldn't walk accrost th street to
pick yew up!' I told her." Max went on. "'Yew kin walk
back to Oklahoma, but wen yew git here I'll be gone.'
That's what I told her, and I sold the farm to th neighbor,
paid everybody else off, an left town. An I ain't bin back
since. I don't know what happened to her after I filed fer

th divorce and I come down here to git me some distance." Max told that story a few times over the months they worked together, and Hector figured he still needed to remind himself he was right to leave her behind and find a new life.

It was a tale that Hector understood, and each time it was repeated he pretended that Max hadn't told him the story before.

And while Max was making a lot less money in Sonora than he could have made north of the border, he still found the time to be generous. One day Hector saw him bargaining with a couple of ladies from the local Seri village for some shell and bone bracelets they had made, and that he didn't really need. Then he paid them, and they walked away giggling.

Max turned to Hector and laughed as he said, "They wanted 300 pesos but I got em down to *quinientos* pesos an a box of oat bars fer their children."

Hector knew that Max was well aware that *quinientos* meant 500, but he was a generous guy that way. He was making plenty of money to live a good life in Tiburón, because the rent was low and food prices were cheap. And Hector's old fishing buddies were aways happy to share part of their catch. It was a very good life for Max, and for Hector, and Max didn't mind sharing some of his good fortune.

Max never quite got the Spanish-speaking ability, but he and Hector seemed to communicate well enough, and Hector learned a lot of English. At least he hoped it was good English, although Max seemed to have his own way of speaking it.

Don Abelardo wore the newest and shiniest boots in town, and they looked expensive. "But them ain't workin' boots," Max told Hector. "Them's hang around the dance hall boots. They're jist fer show." He was proud of his own well-worn footwear and he said, "These here boots has seen some work, an' they show it. They're well-worn-in now an' they may not look good or smell real good, but they're real comfortable and reliable."

Don Abelardo would come by occasionally to check on the progress of their work, but mostly he left them alone. When Max addressed him as Don Abelardo, the "Lardo" part seemed to be more heavily accented than it should be, and Don Abelardo, who understood English pretty well and was more overweight than he should be, graciously smiled and ignored it.

Fresas con crema, a bowl of sliced strawberries covered with cream and sugar, was one of Max's favorite treats, but he called it *frescas con crema*, like the soft drink. He never got the pronunciation right, and it didn't really matter to Hector. *"No me importa,"* he said. But it seemed to annoy Bess, the gringa who taught Spanish classes to the expats. And Hector sometimes thought Max did it just to annoy her. It was one of the many laughs they shared to make a long working day in the hot sun seem short, and Hector really enjoyed hanging out with the big gringo.

And yet, each day Hector saw the guys he used to go fishing with in their pangas as they left Tiburón and headed outbound toward the plentiful harvest of the Sea. Even though he'd made the choice to be land-bound for now, he still felt that he was part of that life—that *cofradía*—that brotherhood. It would be in his blood forever. And every evening he parked The Beast on a hill overlooking the Sea, as if it too were longing for the water. Or at least watching over the safe return of those other young men of the Sea.

While Hector always felt the call of the Sea, he remembered his time working with the big gringo as some of the best years of his life.

Until that day when the peso collapsed and Don Abelardo went bust overnight. He awoke one morning to find that 90% of his money had evaporated when the government announced a ten-to-one readjustment of the peso to the US dollar. There was no money left to pay the bills, and Max had to leave town, with his small stash of now-devalued pesos, to cross the border and find another job back in the US. The other workers scrambled to haul off stacks of concrete blocks, and bags of cement, and whatever assets they could carry away as partial payment of their unpaid wages. And that's how Hector ended up with The Beast, *la bestia*, the bulldozer.

With the big machine, he still managed to make a modest living clearing and leveling for local people and for the gringos who were now buying most of the lots along the beach at the new and cheaper prices. And Don Abelardo let him continue to park The Beast on the unsold hill lot that overlooked the Sea. It was parked there facing out across the ocean, he told his friends, as his talisman— his guardian, to watch over him whenever he went out for a day on the water with his Tio Alfredo or his old fishing buddies. The huge machine, *la bestia*, would always be there, watching for his return.

The late-night rapping at his door woke Hector and he quickly put on a shirt. He opened the door and saw his fishing buddy Mario standing in the shadows just outside.

"Come on," he said, "there's a big load on the beach and we need your help."

Hector donned the rest of his clothes, along with his rubber boots and waterproof jacket, because he knew it would be a cold boat ride and a long night. It took about an hour under a moonless sky for Mario's panga to round the last point along the coast to where they could barely make out an old repurposed jet airliner mired in the sand on a remote beach in the Sea of Cortez. It was the biggest airplane Hector had ever seen, and it was hard to imagine that this one-time modern marvel that had recently been sold for scrap was so quickly repurposed for a midnight delivery.

There were several big pangas with powerful engines nosed up onto the shore with their anchors buried in the dunes. And there was a bunch of guys with the pangas that Hector did not know. They were heavily armed. They were barking orders at the local workers, and Hector was cautious not to stare at any of them. It would be a long night of heavy work as they hauled dozens of plastic-wrapped bales and boxes from the interior of the old gutted airliner. One by one, they filled the big pangas and watched them speed northward, up the Sea of Cortez, into the blackness of night.

It was still an hour or two before dawn when the loading was finished. Then one of the armed men handed Mario a bag of money and told them all to get lost. They quickly shoved their panga into the water and headed back to Tiburón to arrive in the darkness well before the sun rose, and before there would be suspicions afoot, although most people in Tiburón knew it was best not to question what happened on the Sea during the darkest nights.

Hector had done this before. It paid very well—at least a month's wages in one long back-breaking night of work, and he was always on board whenever Mario needed a reliable hand. But he knew not to talk about it. He also understood that they had left several bales and bags strewn around the interior of the plane and on the beach so that the Mexican army would have at least some evidence to show at the coming press conference that would be publicized on TV and in the newspapers. That was the usual arrangement, and the reason the Army did not show up as soon as they knew the plane had landed. Everybody understood. During the next month, the old airliner would be cut apart into scrap metal and hauled away. And Hector knew that all of this was mostly for the entertainment of the US taxpayers, the ones who were paying for this whole charade.

Alberto, Roberto, Gilberto and Filiberto—"*los quatro Bertos*," they called themselves—were brothers who lived in Hermosillo, and they built a house together on one of Don Abelardo's best beach lots in Tiburón for their families to share. There were plenty of bedrooms, and four garages—two on each side of the main entry door. They came out to Tiburón often to go fishing, although Gilberto was usually happy to stay behind and enjoy some quiet family time on the beach. Hector took the other three out fishing when he could wrangle a panga from one of his cousins for the day, and he knew where the best fishing holes were.

Sometimes their *machismo* prevailed and they stayed out longer than they should have and got caught in a nasty blow or two. But Hector had a deep understanding of the Sea and its many moods. And they had always made it back to port with stories of adventures to tell their family and friends over numerous beers, or icy cold margaritas at a local taqueria.

They often recalled a favorite tale about a *niebla fuerte*, a dense fog, that set in and they couldn't see two meters in front of the boat. Fog is a rare thing on the Sea of Cortez, and a cold dry backwind on a sunny winter's morning had caught them by surprise. After they were blinded by the fog, they realized they should have expected it after that four-day northerly quit blowing down the Sea and the cold air shifted east to filter down through the mountains and over that warm water back in the broad estuary. When that happens you can just watch the cold dry gusts suck water upward from the warm surface of the estuary and turn it into an instant mist. Within a few minutes they were completely engulfed by the fog and were quickly disoriented.

Almost nobody in Tiburón owns a compass for navigation, because there are always mountains and islands to serve as markers. But Hector understood the wave trains generated by the gusts flowing down from the east across that broad plain from Hermosillo, and he pointed their bow directly into the wind and toward that shore. The waves became smaller in the lee of the land,

and as they drew closer, he eased off the throttle to better feel the winds as they backed around the hidden headlands and came over his port bow. The sound of surf came through barely now over the motor noise, and he veered a bit northerly to keep the surf just off his starboard side until they were well beyond the rock-strewn point and bigger waves again crossed their bow. The broad-backed swells now told him they were into deeper water and he could head more directly toward the beach he knew was there, hidden in the fog.

The waves again grew smaller in the lee of the familiar shore, and Hector eased forward slowly to find an open spot between the other pangas that had already run up onto the beach. Then he drifted back out and chose the right moment to gun the throttle so they hit the beach and slid up onto the sand. At the last minute he reached back and pulled up the engine to protect the prop, and then they were safe on the beach again.

There were even more stories to share about that wild adventure they once had coming back from Isla San Esteban and they got caught in a strengthening northerly wind pushing against a strong incoming tide. About twice a day the Pacific tides push enormous amounts of seawater northwesterly into the Sea of Cortez, and then it recedes again twice daily. If there's a strong northerly wind roaring down the Sea over an incoming tide, the waves quickly become huge as they pile up against the wind. That was the condition that had developed as Hector and *los Bertos* began their run for home on that day, and their panga was quickly little more than a toy in the water.

Again, it was Hector who recalled the teachings of his Tio Alfredo and carefully tillered the panga diagonally up the face of each wave to cut through the crest just before it became a plunging breaker, and then again he steered it diagonally down the backside to avoid sticking their bow into the next wave face and swamping the boat. He barked orders at his crew to shift their weight forward or aft, or from one side to the other, as needed to balance the boat, and at least one of them spent his time with a plastic bailing bucket staying just ahead of the water level sloshing over their feet in the bottom of the panga.

Over the course of several exhausting hours Hector got them through the maelstrom and into the wind shadow and calm water on the south side of massive Isla Tiburón where they pulled into the protection of Dog Bay and eased onto the shore behind that large sheltering rock to spend the night. It was a cold night and they were chilled to the bone, but the sheer exhilaration of the day kept them from getting much rest, and they talked around a small fire until dawn, reliving each exciting moment of the trip. They were exhausted by the time they got back to Tiburón in mid-morning the next day.

Over the years they spent on the Sea with Hector, the four Bertos had built an abiding trust in his judgement and looked forward to their weekends away from the pressures of their thriving businesses in Hermosillo. And anytime Hector said it was a good day for fishing they would go back out onto the amazing Sea of Cortez—and ignore any warnings they might hear.

This time, only Alberto and Roberto were in town and they were looking forward to a break from work. They ignored Alma Garcia's warnings about a powerful *norteño,* a cold front that was heading directly down the Sea over the next few days. A lot of things had changed in Tiburón over the years. Some of the parents had been able to pay for high school, and a few of those kids had gone off to college. And many of them only returned for *Semana Santa*, weddings, and other important events. Alma was in school with Hector when they were younger, but she had gone off to study meteorology. After graduation she returned to a job in Tiburón at the Port Captain's office. And now she had a computer where she could watch the forecasts and study large satellite maps.

Her predictions were usually right, and those early winter cold fronts were not to be taken lightly. But sometimes she was not right, and Hector still preferred the traditional *vista de la puerta* method that he'd learned from the older fishermen when he was young. The truth was there in the sky and in the wind, they said, if you knew what to look for. So he stepped from his front door at dawn to read the sky and to understand its message. Then he walked the beach to study the motion of the waves and test the wind. He also recalled those high cirrus clouds that told him yesterday what to expect for today. He knew that the intense sun of Sonora, the great heat engine in the sky, determined how powerful the winds would be. An overcast sky reduced the daily heat from the sun, so he knew the cold winds that drove the big waves would be weaker.

The overcast morning sky told Hector they could launch the boat. There was a breeze coming down the Sea, but it looked manageable, and they did not want to miss a good day on the water. A couple of Hector's buddies helped to push the panga down the sand toward the Sea.

Hector tossed a canvas bag of emergency provisions into the boat, along with a 5-gallon *garafón* of water. Then he climbed in to lower the engine as the stern cleared the beach. Alberto and Roberto loaded a cooler full of beer before they grabbed the bow, pushed the boat out from the shore, and jumped aboard. Hector started the engine, backed away, then pointed the bow out to sea, and they were quickly planing over the water away from the village. Hector glanced at The Beast sitting high on the hill overlooking the water; it was a fine day in early March and he knew everything would be OK.

Alberto and Roberto stayed forward in the panga to hold the bow down as they plunged forward through the waves in the shelter of Isla Tiburón and then across the channel to Isla San Esteban. The salt spray over the bow had a familiar and bracing effect in the chilly morning. Roberto had brought his VHF handheld radio so they could stay in touch with their families, at least as long as they had contact. They had enough provisions onboard and in the cooler in case they had to spend a cold night ashore someplace, and they were ready for yet another adventure to share when they returned.

Alma Garcia watched them depart and felt a foreboding that she did not want to admit, but she knew the

approaching weather would test Hector's abilities more
than she hoped. About an hour later, Roberto called in to
the radio net to tell Alma that the seas were rough and
they had slowed the boat to reduce pounding as they
crossed the broad open channel from Isla Tiburón to San
Esteban, but he felt they were managing well so far.

They reached the lee of San Esteban, where the waves
were not so strong. They spent part of the day slowly
trolling the steep cliff sides, and by the afternoon they had
several good yellowtail aboard the boat. Then the sky
cleared, as the bank of high thin clouds slid off to the east,
and the winds began to grow stronger. The waves between
San Esteban and Tiburón were now building quickly in the
wind, and a crossing back to the bigger island began to
look treacherous. They knew they were going to spend a
night ashore on San Esteban, something they'd done a few
times before over the years. They had a large cooler filled
with sixes of Tecate and Corona for an emergency just like
this, and they were looking forward to this good excuse
for building a driftwood fire by a tall sheltering hillside
and enjoying another night of each other's company far
from the everyday land-bound hassles they loved to
escape. As soon as they found a good landing site.

There's a small spit on the southwest corner of San
Esteban that sometimes provides good protection, but this
time the wind-driven waves were casting spray over the
spit and it wasn't a good place to ride out the blow. So
Hector steered the panga up the easterly side of the island
toward the only other protected spit where the big cleft
between the hills, the broad *arroyo central*, spills out onto
a sandy beach.

These northerly winds of winter are part of the same cold front systems that create the Santana winds that roar down the valleys of California to the Pacific Ocean, and they're also funneled down the Sea of Cortez through the bigger midriff islands like Ángel de la Guarda and Tiburón, flowing in a southeasterly direction. Scientists from the university in Hermosillo have explained the importance of these winter winds to the abundant sea life in the Sea of Cortez because they turn over the water as it rushes in on the higher tides and churn nutrients up from the bottom of the deepest channels to feed the plankton and *sardinas* that are the basis of life in the Sea. So the winds are an important part of life to the fishermen of Tiburón, and to the rich bounty that is the Sea of Cortez.

The easterly side of San Esteban provides a bit of leeward shelter behind a projecting spit of stone that creates a small cove, and that's where Hector and the two Bertos were going to ride this one out. They had to swing wide of the spit to come in on its protected northeastern side, and that took them out briefly into the building waves. Alberto grabbed the bailing bucket and stayed even with the water that crashed over the bow while Hector kept them pointed into the oncoming waves. They rounded the rocky tip into the protection of the spit and beached the boat as far onto the sand as they could. Then they tied two stout lines around a pair of large boulders to keep the boat pointed into the shore and from drifting away. The large colony of *lobos del mar*, the sea lions resting on the rocks nearby, barked their disapproval at this intrusion, as their newborn pups dashed into the water for safety.

Hector saw Anselmo Peralta's panga on the other side of the channel, beyond the highest waves in the center, and he watched as they worked their way carefully down the rugged coast of Isla Tiburón and through the rock-strewn notch inside Isla Turner to seek flat water in the wind shadow of the big island. They could stay there overnight in protected Dog Bay, but Hector guessed they'd make their final run in the moderate waves of late afternoon back to the village, and he wished he'd talked the two Bertos into staying over on that side of the channel. Now they were probably stuck on Isla Esteban until this thing blew itself out, and who knew how long that could take.

Roberto called Alma again on the VHF to say they were doing OK. They planned to hunker down overnight and build a brush shelter under a cliff edge. His radio transmission came in scratchy, but it was legible. Alma had tried calling them when the wind began growing stronger but realized they were probably busy fighting the waves and could not hear her calls. And now she was relieved that they were safely ashore and not trying to cross the channel. She knew they'd be okay if they stayed put, so she wished them well, and asked them to check back with her in the morning.

They found a crude shelter of rock and brush that was built long ago by Hector's Tio Alfredo when he spent a few nights here during another winter storm long ago, and they added a bit more brush to it. Then they lit a small fire in the protected lee of the enclosure, and Alberto hauled three cold beers out of the cooler. As evening settled over the island, they cooked one of the fish they'd caught

earlier and opened a can of *frijoles refritos*. And they each
had another beer.

For these three *compadres* it was a familiar wonderful
feeling to be nestled into their crude little shelter on an
island somewhere out on the great Sea of Cortez and with
no good reason to be going anywhere else for a while.
Large waves were now pounding the shore and sometimes
they shook the very rocks of the little shelter, but the night
was spent in stories and jokes and beer until the three
amigos nodded off around the dying fire.

The morning broke clear and it was still windy, and they
cooked up another piece of fish for breakfast. There was
dust in the air as the winds seemed to increase, and large
waves were still marching down the strait between them
and Isla Tiburón. They checked the lines that were still
holding the boat safely in the cove and then called in to
Alma. She could just make out that they were staying on
the island for now. They had everything they needed for at
least a few days and later they'd look over the situation
before making a decision.

It was going to be a long day of waiting on the island,
so they walked up the arroyo to a place where they could
climb onto a ridge and look outward to the north, into the
wind. They passed a big chuckwalla lounging on a warm
rock in a protected sunny spot, and he watched them go
by. Hector was always amazed at how colorful the
chuckwallas were on San Esteban.

As they stood on the windy ridge, they saw endless
whitecaps to the north stretching to distant Isla Ángel de la
Guarda. To the east the waves washed along the cliffs of Isla

Tiburón, the largest island, and to the west lay Isla San Lorenzo, with the infamous Canal de Salsipuedes beyond. Hector was glad he'd never been caught in the channel they called *salsipuedes*, which translates to "get out if you can." The very name implies that when the conditions get bad it's already too late to start thinking about leaving. His Tio Alfredo had told him of the vertical waves that build in that channel when a fierce northerly meets a strong incoming tide, and he shared tales of the panga fishermen that he knew who had died there when their pangas were smashed by those towering monsters. And maybe even Hector's father, who had never returned from working in Guerrero Negro. That channel was deadly in these conditions, but the white-flecked channel he was watching now—the one they would have to cross eventually, the one between San Esteban and Tiburón—was bad enough.

Hector and the two Bertos spent the rest of the day mostly napping, gathering driftwood and small branches for the evening fire, and hanging around their little campsite. In the evening after dinner they enjoyed a few more beers, and fish, and beans; and Hector wandered away from the fire to find an open sandy spot in the arroyo to lie on his back and watch the stars wheel across the sky. He felt guilty for his arrogance—for disregarding Alma's warning—and he was troubled by the realization that soon he was going to have to make a critical decision, as the wind showed no sign of abating. And he needed some quiet time alone. In the distance he could hear Alberto and Roberto laughing together at whatever joke or funny story they had just shared. They were the oldest of the four brothers, and they had always been the closest.

Hector watched Orion, the big winter constellation, as it rose in the east. The stars were more brilliant here than under the streetlights back in the village where he hardly ever noticed them, and out here they felt closer to the earth. They almost seemed to roar with a cosmic fire as they burned forever in the deep black night sky. To the north was *La Osa Mayor*, the one the gringos called The Big Dipper. His buddy, Max the mechanic, had told him that his Irish relatives called it The Starry Plough. And it did look like one of those crude old plows, he thought, that the oxen used to pull through the fields at little ranchos in the Sierra east of Hermosillo. And no matter what terrible thing was happening down here on this planet, those stars up there never even seemed to notice.

The next morning again dawned clear and windy, although the winds had decreased a bit during the night. The early morning waves appeared to be smaller but there was no sign that the winds were about to die down. It was hard to tell from standing here on the Isla what the waves were really like out in the open and exposed center of the channel, and Hector knew the winds would increase after the sun—the big heat engine—was again high in the sky. He decided to wait another day, and Roberto radioed that message to Alma. But the battery was running low on his VHF and he wasn't sure the message got sent.

Alma got a garbled and broken message, and she thought—she hoped—that Hector was going to stay on the island, because that big cold winter low pressure center far to the north had stalled and the wind forecast was bad for at least another day or so. And that's what she said into her radio, but she got no response and she didn't know if the message got through. She wasn't normally a religious person, and neither was Hector, but now she prayed to San Andrés, Hector's patron saint and the patron saint of fishermen, and she asked for his protection, as a special favor.

After yet another day on the island Alberto was ready to leave, and he said so that night around the campfire. Roberto had been expecting this from his impatient brother, and he'd been trying to keep enough battery power on the radio if he needed it to call in to the village to let them know when the decision was made. He asked Alberto to sleep on it until the morning and discuss it then, but he knew when Alberto made a decision it would be difficult to change his mind.

The waves pounded all night again on the rocky shores and steep cliffs of Isla Esteban, as the sea lions barked, and Hector found it difficult to sleep. He knew the dangers of trying to fight their way through heavy waves in a panga that had no flotation and carried a heavy engine. There was no room for a single mistake that could swamp the boat and carry them quickly to the bottom. He tried to imagine what his Tio Alfredo would do—what he had actually done each time over the years when he was faced with a situation like this. He had aways returned because he was careful. He was not a boastful man and he never said he had outsmarted the weather, or the fates, or any kind of god. He had waited patiently for the winds to die, no matter how long it took, if the fates willed it. And now he was still a member of the community. And those others —those impetuous others—were gone.

Hector knew that Alberto and Roberto honored and respected his abilities on the Sea. But Alberto was the president of a large company in Hermosillo, and he was used to giving orders, and to having them obeyed. But that's not how things work in the natural world, and Hector well knew the consequences of rash behavior on the sea. Especially on this particular part of the Sea.

The Sea of Cortez is sheltered by the long Baja Peninsula from the constant waves of the Pacific and it often appears to be a calm body of water, almost like a big lake. The Baja is a thousand miles long and gives good protection from those wind-driven Pacific rollers that come all the way from Asia to crash on the West Coast. But the Sea of Cortez has its own peculiar climate that creates a different sort of weather. The mountains of the Baja Peninsula may protect it from the Pacific, but they also funnel the fierce northerly winds of winter into powerful gales that rip down the Sea, turning it into an unforgiving maelstrom. It's a fair warning to those who will listen. But Hector was afraid that Alberto would not listen, and he wasn't sure how to handle the decision that he knew was coming.

Hector slept poorly that night, as he listened to Alberto tossing on the hard sand and rocks trying to find a way to get comfortable. He was also aware that Roberto was quietly watching his brother, as the last embers faded in the fire pit, and hoping he would relax.

Waves crashed again onto the shore all night, the wind swirled through their brush shelter, and they got little rest as they each pondered the morning to come. Hector arose early as the pre-dawn gloom slowly filled the broad arroyo and he stoked a new fire to make another breakfast of fish and beans and instant coffee. Alberto and Roberto soon joined him by the fire to warm up after another cold night on the sand, and they choked down yet more of the same fare they'd been eating since they arrived on San Esteban. Hector had grown up with this sort of life and he was used to it, but for the Bertos, what had begun as an adventure—as a lark—had started to resemble drudgery.

Back home in Hermosillo the Bertos each slept on fine linens and had cooks who brought breakfast to the table. Neither of their wives really knew how to cook and their children were growing up with those same expectations of privilege. Alberto's lavish *casona,* in the elite *Pitic* part of town, even had two kitchens. There was the gorgeous show kitchen, where his wife Elena could set out cups for tea and little plates for the fancy cakes she bought for gatherings with her lady friends. And just behind a connecting door, there was a large and functional kitchen where their old live-in cook, Maria Luz, did the real work of providing food for the family.

The four Bertos had grown up in a prominent and well-to-do family, one that even included a few mayors and a state governor, and they had all been to the best schools. And now they loved getting away from that pampered life occasionally and pretending to be part of the *gente*, the common people. But after a few days of misery out on a cold desert island, this affectation of commonality with the poor had gotten old. And Alberto, especially, was recalling the comfort of his nice home in town, and even the luxury of that cruise ship he'd taken the family on recently in the warm Caribbean.

Soon the rising sun flashed its golden glow upon the peak of the large hill nearest to them and its light began creeping down the slope to replace the grey and somber hues of early morning with the vivid colors of the day. And for the moment they put off having yet another tasteless breakfast of mostly beans and some fish that was starting to taste nasty. They walked over to where the boat was still lashed to the boulders and stared silently out at the grey-bearded breakers that were still marching down the Sea in an endless procession. The boat rocked from side to side whenever the remains of a large wave raced up the beach and slapped its stern, but it was doing okay just as they had lashed it, and they each waited for someone else to say something. Hector stared toward the bow of the boat where Alma's name was still written in large letters. He didn't want to do something that would disappoint her.

Hector took a deep breath, and said, "I don't know. It still looks rough out there. Maybe it will settle down in a little bit." He was surprised when those words came out of his mouth, because he had something of a reputation for being headstrong and taking chances. And he didn't want to admit he was thinking again of Alma. But he knew it was unlikely the waves would decrease, and he knew the heat of the rising sun would keep the cold wind coming.

It was all about temperature differential. That's how he remembered the way Alma explained it after she got back from college. "The clearer the sky, the hotter the sun will cook the inland desert floor and cause the air to rise. And then the colder the air that comes from the north to replace it, the harder the wind will blow," she had said. "And as long as we have a large difference in the two temperatures, the wind will keep blowing. And it will blow for several days, until that changes."

Hector knew she was right, although he wanted to believe something would change soon and they could get back to the village. He also didn't want to think about Alma. That was over now, and he had changed a lot since their early days together.

Alma had also changed when she went off to college. Over the many times she returned to Tiburón she had introduced Hector to poetry and other things, and he was fascinated by the knowledge bound into a book that he could hold in his hand. He was especially interested in the rationalism of Spinosa and his focus on the scientific method. It was a philosophy that had gotten the young Spinosa into deep trouble long ago, and Hector could relate to that. As he looked at the wind-tossed Sea he wondered what secrets the science of weather and ocean had to tell him.

Their lives were no longer the same as before, when Alma and he were in classes at the *secundaria*. She was always a bright spark in school, a *chispa*, and she had gone onward to the *prepa* when she was 15 with the help of a local gringo couple; but Hector had gone to work. Max once told him that high school was free in the United States, and he found it hard to believe that a higher level of school could be free for poor kids like himself. Nobody in his family had ever told him such a thing and maybe none of them even knew that. But none of them had ever been past *secundaria* either.

After her college years, when Alma finally returned to live again in Tiburón, she mentioned an opera called "La Forza del Destino" by some Italian guy, that she had seen in her college classes in Hermosillo. She said the story was different with her and Hector, but the message was the same. It was their destiny to take different pathways in the world, and now they would always be different people from when they were young.

Hector thought it was strange that he would think of that as he looked out over a turbulent Sea that might be the major turning point in his life, a point beyond which he may never return. Like the Gates of Hell from Dante, that the old priest had often spoken of at mass when Hector was young, and those terrifying latin words that hung over the Gate: "Lasciate ogni speranza voi ch'entrate." Although Hector thought that he did not really believe in that stuff any more, it still haunted him as he faced the treacherous waters that now beckoned him to what could well be his final destiny.

Alberto looked over at Hector for an uncomfortable amount of time, and then he looked back at the Sea. Roberto watched them both to see what the next move was going to be. Hector had felt Alberto staring at him but he kept his eyes on the Sea, studying its moods and the way it may have changed over the night. Alberto may be the boss, but he knew nothing of the Sea. Then Alberto swore at the Sea and turned back to their campsite to stoke up another fire to heat some more beans.

Alberto was sick of eating refried beans and he was actually glad they only had a few cans left. He was to the point of thinking that sticks and twigs might even taste better than any more of those beans. But the time had come to make some kind of decision, and he wasn't going to wait much longer.

Hector stayed by the boat to study the raging Sea and ponder those bleak words written by Dante over the gates of Hell so many centuries ago, "Abandon hope, all ye who enter here." And he recalled that Alma had once quoted Nietzsche, from a philosophy class she'd taken, "Only great pain is the ultimate liberator of the spirit." Hector had matured since his early reckless years and now he had little interest in adding more pain to the vagaries of his daily life. There was plenty of pain around without looking for more.

He knew they should wait on the island and hope for better conditions in a few days, but they were low on food and water and a decision would be coming soon. He watched the endless whitecaps as the gusting winds still roared out of the Northwest, and he knew that soon they'd be battling the biggest waves in the center of the channel. And that coming passage back to the mainland would be the most important test of his life.

Time passes slowly in a small Mexican beach town. The seasons come and the seasons go, as the winds and the tides. People tend to the constant important needs of their daily lives. People forget.

Two years had passed since Hector made his run from the island for the mainland. Tio Alfredo was staring out at the Sea of Cortez, as he often did after that day when Hector and his boat failed to return—that day when he disappeared somewhere out there in the turbulent waters. Tio Alfredo had not forgotten, and the heartbreak and pain of losing his favorite *sobrino* would forever be with him. But he knew the time had come to move beyond it. Don Abelardo had quietly mentioned that he needed to sell that hilltop lot, where The Beast was stored, to one of the new gringos in town. He had refused to sell it since the tragedy but now he needed to recover some of the money he'd lost when they devalued the peso. It had been several tough years, and now he wanted to move on.

Tio Alfredo agreed that it was time to move forward, for himself and for the community. The Sea gives, and the Sea takes away. It had always been the bargain of the life he'd lived, that the Sea will demand its full payment some day, and someone will have to pay back. And this time it was Hector.

Nobody really knew what happened after that last scratchy call from the island when they appeared to say they were leaving the sheltered shore and making a run for the village. Nobody could know what happened out there in the storm; but when they didn't return, Tio Alfredo could picture everything that might have happened when they hit the big water in the channel. And he ran it through his mind often, searching for answers that he knew he'd never find. The panga was tough enough for the worst of it, and the engine was reliable. But there were still so many variables that nothing of what happened in those last minutes and hours of their lives could be known for certain.

As long as the engine kept running and Hector carefully climbed the backs of the huge waves as they marched southward on the wind, and if he dodged all of the breaking crests that could fill the boat quickly, and if they weren't hit by one of the occasional larger rogue waves, to be pitch-polled into the trough ahead of it —if all of that worked out just right, they might have made it through. But something terrible happened out there on that remorseless Sea.

There might have been rust or dirt that came loose in their fuel tank in the pounding waves and clogged the fuel line to stop the reliable beat of the big engine. They may have caught a piece of drifting fishing line that was picked up by the waves and then jammed the propeller, and that could have stopped the engine. That channel between the islands is over a thousand feet deep and nobody keeps crab traps out there, but maybe one came loose from the shallow water near the island to be carried on the wind and the strong currents, and they had the bad luck to snag it. Or maybe it was a piece of drift net lost out there by a careless trawler crew. The Sea is a dangerous place, and anything can happen. And if the engine quit under those conditions it would be a catastrophe for them.

All these possibilities and more had been on Tio Alfredo's mind even while they were still safely on the island. He knew that if anything went wrong and the engine stopped on such a bad passage, the heavy engine at the stern would drag like a storm anchor and then the wind would catch the light bow of the boat like a sail to swing it around, pointing it downwind. And that would expose the low stern of the boat directly to the waves.

Then the next large breaker could easily swamp the boat, and probably much faster than they could bail it out. And if not that wave, then one of the many others behind it that came endlessly down the Sea that day. One of the big breakers would sink them, and that now-dead heavy engine that had been their only hope of survival would pull Hector's panga to the bottom.

The fishermen of the village looked for clues when they found Roberto's body floating in his lifejacket. And a few days later Alberto's bloated body washed ashore in tranquil Dog Bay, carried by the swirling currents that sweep through the Sea twice a day. *Pero, los muertos no hablan,* and dead men keep their secrets. It's the ancient code of the fisherman, and he accepts the way his cards are dealt. If it is God's Will, *si Dios quiere*, I'll return to my family. And if not, *a mi me toca*, it's my turn to pay the toll.

Over the following week, they found two more empty lifejackets that had been aboard the boat. One had been badly torn, as if it had gotten tangled in a final struggle to save the boat, to maybe free the propeller. But nobody could ever know for certain what had really happened out there. And they never found the body of Hector.

Alma stopped to lean on the heavy blade of the big bulldozer that was still sitting there on the hill overlooking the ocean. It was facing the sparkling waters of the Sea of Cortez, and she shared a final view with Tio Alfredo and the old rusted machine that now seemed beaten and forlorn. She passed it each day on her way to work, and it brought a tear to her eyes yet again as she stood with it and thought of what might have been. La Bestia was just as Hector had left it, as a *talismán*, a guardian to keep watch over him, when she begged him not to go out into the storm. And when he disappeared in the waves, his uncle Alfredo had left it there as a memorial for his favorite *sobrino*—and as a reminder to the other young guys who went out there every day and who might be thinking they were tougher and smarter than the Sea. It was the Sea that gave them life, but it demanded their respect and it was always willing to harvest the arrogant ones among them.

And now it was the duty of Tio Alfredo to move the old bulldozer, as Don Abelardo had requested. The heavy old Beast had been sitting abandoned on the hill, and it took most of a day to get it running again. At last a large black cloud of smoke rose from the exhaust pipe, then Tio Alfredo slipped it slowly into gear. He drove it down onto the vast salt flats just behind the high beach-side dune. It was a place of vestigial mangroves where there had once been a deep estuary maybe a million years ago, but that had been cut off by the dune of drift sand that created the current shore. As he eased the big machine onto the salty flats, he felt the ancient crust breaking beneath its heavy tracks; and he kept going forward until The Beast wallowed in the muck. Then Tio Alfredo stopped the engine and stepped from the cab onto the cracking ground, and he walked away into a setting sun as the huge machine broke fully through the crust and settled slowly into the bottomless mire below.

†††

Perry Robert Wilkes

Author Perry Robert Wilkes lived in New Mexico's beautiful Rio Grande Valley for fifty years. He holds a Bachelor of Arts degree from the School of Architecture at the University of New Mexico and specializes in passive solar residential design and energy efficiency.

His writings on culture, urban issues, architecture, and sailing have been published in the *New Mexico Independent*, *Century Magazine*, the *RGSC Foghorn* — and even include an Op-Ed in the *Albuquerque Journal!*

Wilkes travels by bus or rail in Mexico, South America, the Russian Far East, and Europe, meeting local people on various forms of public transportation, while photographing and writing about his travels.

His in-depth travel dispatches are found online at: https://dispatches.wilkeskinsman.com.

He currently resides in a small town in Sonora, Mexico, where the road ends at the fabled Sea of Cortez.

Other books by Perry Robert Wilkes

I Always Meant to Tell You

Under Torn Paper Mountains

available from

Liberación Press
PO Box 6460
Nogales, AZ 85628

Any independent bookseller or
Barnes & Noble and Amazon.com

Printed in the USA
CPSIA information can be obtained
at www.ICGtesting.com
LVHW070037210823
755777LV00031B/574